F4

Worlds Apart

Cedar River Daydreams

9708

Worlds Apart

....

Judy Baer

BETHANY HOUSE PUBLISHERS
MINNEAPOLIS, MINNESOTA 55438

Published by Bethany House Publishers
A Ministry of Bethany Fellowship, Inc.
11300 Hampshire Avenue South
Minneapolis, Minnesota 55438

Printed in the United States of America.

**Library of Congress Cataloging-in-Publication
Data**

CIP Data applied for

ISBN 1–55661–836–0   CIP

For Misty Nass, my new godchild.
May the Lord bless you always.

JUDY BAER received a B.A. in English and Education from Concordia College in Moorhead, Minnesota. She has had over forty novels published and is a member of the National Romance Writers of America, the Society of Children's Book Writers, and the National Federation of Press Women.

Two of her novels, *Adrienne* and *Paige*, have been prizewinning bestsellers for Bethany House. Both books have been awarded first place for juvenile fiction in the National Federation of Press Women's communications contest.

Facts about the
Republic of Greece:

—includes mainland Greece and hundreds of Greek
  islands
—is located in southeastern Europe
—is bordered by three seas: the Ionian, the Aegean,
  and the Mediterranean
—has Athens as its capital
—has as its flag a white cross on a blue field
—uses the drachma as its currency
—has a President, a Premier, and Parliament
—uses the metric system
—produces grapes, raisins, figs, olives, fruits,
  grains, and cotton

Chapter One

"Wait till you hear what happened to us last night!" Todd Winston's dark blond hair was messed up, and Lexi Leighton could tell he'd been running. Todd rarely got rattled, so whatever his news, it must be big.

But before she could ask what had happened, Binky and Egg McNaughton both shoved notebooks into Todd's face. "Did you get the answers to questions seven and nine? None of the rest of us did."

"Some of us didn't even try," Jennifer Golden said lazily. She always pretended that she didn't care how difficult school was for her, but Lexi knew that Jennifer had studied late into the night, since they'd done it together.

Peggy Madison didn't say anything but chewed furiously on the tip of her pencil. Matt Windsor yawned and recrossed his legs, bored with the whole scene.

"Will you quit looking at those work sheets and pay attention for a minute!" Todd demanded.

"You don't have to be such a crank," Binky pouted, looking indignant. She closed her book and gave Todd a self-righteous glare. "This had better be good."

"My parents got this wild phone call out of the blue last night," Todd said.

"An obscene phone call? I knew a guy once who—"

"Not an obscene call, Egg! Pay attention! My parents got a call from an organization called StudentLink. This group arranges for foreign exchange students to come to schools in the United States and also for American students to go abroad. They want my parents to take a foreign exchange student!"

"Take him where?" Binky wrinkled her nose and looked confused. "I don't get it."

"Take him into our home! They want to place a student with us."

"No kidding? He'd live with you? Like he was your brother or something?"

Todd frowned. "I guess so. I never really thought about that, but I suppose Mom and Dad would have to treat him just like they treat Mike and me."

"Why you? Why now?" Lexi asked. "Don't foreign exchange students usually come to schools at the beginning of the year?"

"I thought you had to plan in advance to get a student," Peggy commented. "And fill out forms or something."

Todd nodded. "Usually that's the way it's done, but this student's host family just got transferred. He needs a new home right away. My mom knows the coordinator of the exchange program—they went to college together. She thought of my mom and gave her a call."

"What are you going to do?" Jennifer asked curiously.

"We discussed it last night, and my parents decided to say yes."

Now Todd had everyone's attention.

"Cool! When is he coming?" Peggy asked.

"What does he look like? Is he cute?" Jennifer piped up.

"Jennifer, can't you think of anything but guys?" Binky scolded. "You sound so boy crazy!" She paused, then turned back to Todd. "Is he? Cute, I mean?"

When everyone had stopped laughing, Todd replied, "I don't know. I haven't seen him yet. Besides, I'm probably not a very good judge of what makes a guy 'cute' to you girls anyway. All we've gotten so far is a fax with basic information on it. But we'll find out soon enough. He arrives today!"

"Where is he from?" Lexi asked. "Someplace interesting?"

"And what's his name?" Jennifer added.

"His name is Dmitri Katrakis and he's from Greece."

"Greece? As in *ancient* Greece? And the Greek islands?" Lexi gasped.

"That's the one."

"That's one of the most beautiful places in the whole world!"

"How do you know, Lexi? Have you ever been there?" Egg challenged.

"No, but someday I will. I've read so much about

it. It's full of history, not to mention some pretty spectacular beaches." Lexi sighed. "I can't wait to meet someone who actually lives there!"

"Tell us what you know about him," Jennifer ordered. "How long will he be staying?"

"Six weeks, I think. He's halfway through his program."

"Is that all?" Jennifer sounded disappointed. "We'll hardly get to know him before it's time for him to leave."

"I think it's really exciting. Imagine how much we can learn from him." Binky looked at her brother, who was twirling a clump of his hair with his index finger and looking preoccupied. "And you could use some culture, Egg."

"Me? I'm as cultured as they come!"

Jennifer cut off the rude snorting sound Binky made to say, "I think it'll be nice to have a new man around school." She fluffed her hair.

"Minda Hannaford might want to claim him for herself," Peggy teased, referring to Jennifer's least favorite classmate. "Don't get your hopes up."

"Don't you girls think about anything but guys?" Egg grumbled.

"Why does it bother you if we do?" Jennifer retorted. "You're a guy. Maybe somebody is thinking about you. Right, Angela?"

Everyone turned to Angela Hardy. Egg's girlfriend had been so silent that Lexi had almost forgotten she was there. Angela was usually quiet, but today she'd practically made herself invisible.

"Hmmm? What? Who?"

"Guess she's not thinking about you right now,

Egg," Peggy observed dryly. Angela hadn't heard a thing they'd been saying.

Todd was waiting for Lexi by her locker after school. "Ready to go?"

"I sure am. I've had enough school for one day." Lexi tossed her books into her locker and slammed it shut. "Are we stopping at the Hamburger Shack?"

"I can't tonight. This is the day Dmitri is supposed to arrive."

"I'd almost forgotten! Are you excited?"

"Sort of."

"Sort of? That's not a very enthusiastic answer. I thought you were looking forward to this."

They reached Todd's car, and he opened the passenger door for Lexi.

"I am. I mean, I *was*. It's just . . . now that Dmitri is arriving, it feels a little weird. What if I don't like him? What if he doesn't like *me*?"

"I know what you mean," Lexi admitted. "Remember when my family took in Amanda Remer, the foster girl?"

"How could I forget? That was pretty traumatic."

"Exactly. I had a really hard time having her in the house. Sharing my mom with her was tough for a while," Lexi admitted honestly. "But we worked it out, and when she left, I really missed her.

"But it will be different for you," she added. "Amanda was a mixed-up girl. Dmitri *wants* to be in America."

"You're right," Todd said, sounding relieved. "I've probably been obsessing over nothing. Mike hasn't lived at home for a long time, and I've been used to my space. I was just thinking how weird it will be to have a 'brother' in the house again."

"He's probably as nervous about meeting you as you are to meet him. Besides, I think it's going to be lots of fun."

"Then let's get the fun started. Do you want to go home with me and meet Dmitri? He should be at our house by now."

"All right! Let's go."

———————

When they pulled into the Winstons' driveway, Todd said, "Looks like both Mom and Dad are here. That could mean only one thing." He took a deep breath. "Here goes."

A pile of black and green suitcases filled the entry. A leather backpack leaned against the luggage.

In the living room, Todd's mother and dad were visiting with a handsome, black-haired young man. When Todd and Lexi entered, he jumped to his feet.

Dmitri was six feet tall and well built, with wide shoulders and slim hips. He looked strong and athletic. His dark hair was thick and wiry, cut short and combed back from his face. He had an olive complexion and looked as though he'd spent a lot of time in the sun. When he smiled, beautiful white teeth flashed against his tanned face.

Dmitri was one incredible-looking guy, Lexi decided. A smile tickled the corners of her lips. She could hardly wait to see the responses of the girls at school. This was going to be fun.

Dimples formed in his swarthy cheeks as Dmitri greeted Todd and Lexi with a word that sounded like *kalimera*. Then he shyly dropped his eyes to the floor. "Hello."

"Hi, I'm Todd Winston, and this is Lexi Leighton." Todd stepped forward to shake Dmitri's hand. Much to his surprise, Dmitri embraced him and gave him a kiss on the cheek! As Lexi watched in surprise, he turned and did the same for her.

Seeing the shocked expressions on their faces, Dmitri laughed. "This is how we greet the people who are most important to us—like you, my new brother and his friend!"

Dmitri's enthusiasm was contagious. Soon they were all laughing as he regaled them with the greetings Greek people used.

"My grandfather always says, 'How are you going?' when he greets me. Do you ever say that here in America?"

"No, but we sometimes say, 'What's happening?' " Todd said.

"What's happening?" Dmitri rolled the words off his tongue. "I like it. That's what I'll say to my friends when I go home. What's happening?"

Mrs. Winston touched Todd's arm. "Why don't you show Dmitri to his room? I'll bet he'd like to unpack and get settled. After all, he's going to school in the morning."

"Sure, come on." Todd moved into the hallway and picked up a suitcase. "Your room is next to mine. I think you'll like it here."

———

When Lexi walked through the kitchen door, her mother was on the phone. "Wait, Binky," she was saying, "Lexi just arrived." Mrs. Leighton held out the phone to her daughter.

"Hi, Binky. How are you going?"

"Huh? What's that supposed to mean?" But Binky didn't have time to figure out Lexi's new greeting. "Well, did you meet him? Is he nice? Is he cute? Can he speak English? *Tell me!*"

"He seems very nice, what little I saw of him. Yes, he can speak English because it is taught in schools there. And yes, yes, yes, he is *very* cute."

"Ohhh, I knew it. Wait until Jennifer hears that he's good-looking. And Minda and the Hi-Fives! Those girls are going to devour him!"

Binky gave a deep sigh. "I wish I could go abroad. It must be so exciting to go to a new country and learn all about it. To see the things you've only read about in books."

"Maybe you will someday," Lexi said encouragingly.

"Ha! Me? How could I afford that?" Then Binky's tone brightened. "But I have some good news. My parents have given Egg and me the next best thing!"

"To a trip to Europe? What's that?"

"A computer! Can you believe it?"

Lexi was surprised. The McNaughton family was always short of cash, and a computer was an expensive item.

"My dad *won* it at work! Isn't that great? Now

at least I can get on the Internet and look up different countries. Maybe I'll meet someone, and we can e-mail back and forth—like a pen pal only better!"

"Congratulations!" Lexi was excited for her friend. Binky deserved something special.

"Mom and Dad are going to pay for getting hooked up. I can hardly wait."

"I suppose you'll have to share it with your brother," Lexi said with a chuckle. "Egg isn't going to let you be on it all the time."

"I'm not so sure about that. Egg's not very happy about the computer."

"Why? I thought he'd be the one to love it."

"He wanted them to sell it and put the money down on a car for him. He thinks he needs wheels, not bytes. He's been pouting about it ever since Dad came home with the news."

"He can always ride with Todd."

"I know. But Egg's got his ego tied up in this car thing. Oh well," she added cheerfully. "He'll get over it. And until he does, I'll get all the computer time. I'm taking a class on the Internet and the World Wide Web soon. And as soon as I know how, I'm going to look up Greece. I'll bet there are zillions of websites for Greece. I wonder if I should get a head start by reading some books on ancient Greece." Binky hardly drew a breath as she talked.

"You know what's really neat about our new computer? It has a lot of memory. That's a good thing because . . ."

Lexi closed her eyes and listened. She had a hunch that in the near future she was going to be hearing a lot more about computers than she really wanted to know.

Chapter Two

"Why is there an assembly this morning?" Jennifer grumbled. "I needed that time to finish an assignment. What are they trying to do, get me in trouble?"

"Have you considered that *you* might be responsible for not getting your work done on time?" Minda Hannaford said haughtily as she sailed by with Tressa and Gina Williams in tow. The Hi-Fives were a group of girls with highly elevated opinions of themselves.

Jennifer's lip curled. Lexi could practically hear her growl as she turned around.

"Don't let her get to you," Lexi advised. "That will make her morning."

"Why does she get under my skin like that?" Jennifer asked as she and Lexi made their way to the gymnasium.

"Because you let her." Lexi understood how Jennifer was feeling. Minda could bug her, too. The girl had it down to an art form. Minda had problems of her own, and sometimes she brought them to school with her.

Jennifer shook herself. "Got it. Stay cool. What

is this assembly about, anyway?"

"I don't know. I overslept this morning and didn't get here till a couple minutes ago. Have you seen Todd?"

"No. Egg and Binky walked into the school with me, though. Binky was rambling about hard drives and modems and computer whatsits and widgets. The more she talked, the gloomier Egg looked. What's going on with them?"

Briefly, Lexi explained the computer-versus-car controversy at the McNaughton house.

Jennifer whistled. "No wonder! I suppose Egg's been dreaming of wheels, not keyboards. Hi, Angela!"

Angela didn't look any happier than she had the other night, but she fell into step with the two girls.

They walked together into the gymnasium. A podium with a blue and white flag displayed on its front stood facing the bleachers. Egg, Binky, Tim Anders, Matt Windsor, and Anna Marie Arnold were seated together. Binky stood up and waved.

"Have *you* seen Todd?" Jennifer asked when they reached their friends.

"No. It's weird. He's always around by now . . . there he is!" Binky pointed across the gymnasium at Todd, who was standing with Mrs. Waverly and a dark-haired guy wearing a white sweater and black pants.

"Who's *that*?" Binky nearly slipped off the bleacher in her excitement. "He's gorgeous!"

Anna Marie nodded in enthusiastic agreement.

"That's Dmitri, the foreign exchange student," Lexi whispered as Todd, Dmitri, and the principal walked toward the podium.

"I feel an urge to study Greece coming on," Jennifer sighed. "Do you think he'd be my tutor?"

"Shhh. They're going to introduce him."

After a few words from the principal, introducing Dmitri Katrakis and explaining that he would be with them for the next six weeks, Dmitri himself stepped forward. He gave the microphone a quizzical glance before looking up to give the group a dazzling smile. Lexi could practically hear girls melting all over the auditorium.

"I am pleased to be here," Dmitri said in flawless but accented English. "I hope that I will get to meet all of you before I must leave. I will be happy to answer any questions you have about my country."

"He's *mine*," Lexi heard whispered above her. She turned to see who was talking.

"Forget it," Minda hissed to Tressa. "Hands off. I get him first."

Lexi's eyes widened. The Hi-Fives were already plotting and scheming over Dmitri! She shook her head. Those girls were incorrigible.

But Lexi couldn't concentrate on Minda and company because Dmitri was speaking.

". . . can always see the mountains," he was saying. "And in Greece we are never far from the sea. My country is so beautiful, filled with sunlight, mountains, rich valleys—all bound by our picturesque coastline.

"You see, we are surrounded by three seas, the Aegean, the Ionian, and the Mediterranean, and those seas hold hundreds of Greek Islands. As a result, Greeks love the sea. We travel a great deal by the sea in *caïques* (pronounced Ki-yak). These are boats with sails or motors that carry people or produce from island to island. There are also ships and ferries between the mainland and the islands."

Dmitri smiled wistfully. "The beauty is so great that it is difficult for me to express it. There are big cities like Athens and Thessaloniki, as well as ten thousand small Greek villages. I am very proud to have Greece as my home."

When Dmitri was done speaking, students came forward from the bleachers to ask him questions. The Hi-Fives pressed their way into the center.

"I wonder if they'd be so curious about Greece if he weren't so cute?" Binky muttered.

"Do you think he'd tutor me in world history?" Jennifer looked dreamy.

"Is this what we're going to hear for the next six weeks?" Egg groused. "I don't see what's so special about him. What's he got that I don't?"

Egg's ears began to grow red as the girls turned to stare at him. Scrawny, all arms, legs, and Adam's apple, Egg was as different from Dmitri as, well . . . Lexi couldn't even think of a comparison.

Todd joined them then, saving Egg from the inevitable ribbing he was about to get.

"Sorry you can't get to Dmitri. Looks like he's going to be very popular. Don't worry. I'll introduce you all later."

"Is he nice?" Peggy asked.

"So far he's been great. Polite. Cheerful. Like Dmitri himself says, 'No worries.' "

"I'm so glad!" Lexi said with relief in her voice.

Todd put his arm around her shoulders and gave

her a squeeze. "Why don't all of you meet us after school. We'll pile into my car and show Dmitri around Cedar River."

"It's a date," Egg said cheerfully. "I want to get to know this guy better—and to find out what these girls see in him."

———————

Lexi, Jennifer, Peggy, Egg, and Binky found Todd and Dmitri in the video arcade next to the Hamburger Shack. Matt and Tim were there, too, absorbed in a game.

"Here they are," Todd announced to Dmitri. "Now I can introduce you to my friends." He reached out to Lexi. "First of all, you remember Lexi Leighton. She is—"

"Very beautiful." Dmitri touched a strand of silky hair that lay on her shoulder. "Very."

Todd looked amused at Lexi's surprise. "One thing Dmitri isn't lacking is charm."

"I see that." Lexi blushed.

"Lexi has a little brother. His name is Ben, and he's a great kid. I'm sure you'll meet him before you leave."

Todd pointed to his friends one by one. "Binky and Egg McNaughton are brother and sister. They're . . ." Todd searched for words to describe the pair but couldn't find them. When he turned to Jennifer and Peggy, they were both staring with love-sick expressions at Dmitri. One flash of his dazzling white smile and they were both blown away.

Lexi could understand her friends' responses.

Not only was Dmitri incredible looking, but he was friendly, charming, and had a way of making a girl feel as if she were the only person in the universe. Without thinking, she blurted, "Are all Greeks as charming as you?"

Todd looked shocked, and Dmitri burst out laughing. "Thank you!" The smile lines around his eyes deepened. "The Greeks are a very warm and friendly people. You like this?"

Now Lexi was laughing, too. "Very much. I wanted to ask you about—"

A piercing voice broke into Lexi's thought. "Aren't you going to introduce *us* to Dmitri? I'm sure he wants to meet *us*."

"Yeah," Egg muttered at the sound of Minda's voice. "About as much as he wants to meet a bad case of the flu."

Dmitri looked confused at Egg's response to the attractive, well-dressed blond girl bearing down on them, with several friends in tow.

"The Hi-Fives," Binky groaned. "Not them. Not now."

"What are 'high fives'?"

"It's a group of girls who've got this little club going on. They are really good friends and—"

"There's no use explaining any more, Todd," Lexi broke in. "Dmitri will find out for himself soon enough."

It was no use, anyway. Minda Hannaford, Gina and Tressa Williams, and Rita Leonard were already circling Dmitri, looking him over.

Minda was her usual well-dressed self in slim black pants and black chunky-heeled shoes. Her top was a midriff-skimming T-shirt of stretchy ribbed fabric. The other girls were not-quite-so-pulled-together clones of Minda's look. No matter what else the Hi-Fives were—stuck up, snooty, self-absorbed—they definitely kept up with the latest styles.

Dmitri's eyebrows were inching higher in concern as the girls eyed him. Then Minda thrust out her hand.

"I'm Minda Hannaford. I write the fashion column for the *Cedar River Review*. Welcome to our school." Then she actually batted her eyelashes! "We want to know absolutely *everything* about your country. We'll have to get to know each other."

At least Minda had the good sense not to add *very well* to her statement.

The other girls were equally nauseating, Lexi observed with amusement. Gina and Tressa got a fit of the giggles that made their faces turn red. Rita was totally tongue-tied. They all acted like immature pre-teens fawning over a teenage rock star. The way things were stacking up, Dmitri's visit was going to be very interesting.

Finally, it was Jennifer's not-too-discreet half giggle, half groan that broke up the little circle of fans around Dmitri.

"They're making me sick," Jennifer muttered. "Why can't those girls leave any decent guy alone?" Then she grinned. "So I can have first chance at him!"

"Oh, you are hopeless!" Lexi growled, but she wasn't angry. This entire situation was getting more hilarious by the minute.

One by one the others had to go, finally leaving just Todd, Dmitri, Binky, Egg, Jennifer, and Lexi.

"Now that there are only six of us left, we'll all fit into my car. Let's give Dmitri a tour of his new home for the next six weeks."

As they approached Todd's old 1949 coupe, Dmitri burst into laughter. At the others' questioning glances, he explained, "This was a most unexpected car for me to find Todd driving. I thought all Americans drove big, flashy cars, and then I find"—he gestured expansively—"this!"

Todd loved his old car. He was into vintage vehicles because he could restore them at his brother Mike's garage. He didn't apologize for the car. "Just wait until you feel how it hugs the road and how it drives. This is a great car. It's built like a tank. Nothing better on country roads. You'll see."

They piled inside.

"Move over, Egg, you're blocking my view." Binky gave her brother an elbow in the arm.

"You don't need to see anything. You live here. What do you care as long as Dmitri gets a window? And quit poking those knobby elbows at me. They should be registered as weapons."

"And your elbows are so special? Hah! You could dial a telephone with yours. Or type on a computer, or . . ."

"You'll get used to it," Todd said with a sigh to Dmitri. "Egg and Binky do this all the time. We just ignore it until we can't stand it anymore. Then we make them quit."

Dmitri smiled broadly. "It's okay. Family is very important to the Greeks. We like being together, but sometimes we sound like Binky and Egg, too."

"Nobody sounds quite like them," Jennifer assured him. "But it's nice of you to be so polite."

"Where should we go first?" Todd asked.

"The museum," Lexi suggested.

"The mall, of course," Jennifer said.

"And you've got to drive by The Station." Binky was referring to Cedar River's most elite restaurant, the one decorated to resemble the gracious dining cars on turn-of-the-century trains.

"Okay, and if you think of other things along the way, let me know." Todd shifted into gear and they were off.

Unfortunately, Cedar River's museum was closed because the dinosaur display that was opening the following week was being assembled. The mall, on the other hand, was so enticing that they decided to set an entire day aside to visit it so that Dmitri could do some "serious shopping."

"If you turn here," Lexi suggested, "we'll go right by my dad's clinic."

"Your father is a doctor?" Dmitri sounded impressed.

"A veterinarian, actually."

"I see."

"Would you like to stop and say hello?" Lexi asked. "I'm sure he wouldn't mind."

They piled out of the car in front of the light brick building with its brown cedar-shake roof and brown shutters. Lexi led the way inside.

Her father was standing in the waiting room, holding a Dalmatian puppy and visiting with its owner.

"Hello, kids. What's up?"

"This is Dmitri, the foreign exchange student who's living at Todd's house. We're just showing him the town. Oh, Dad, that puppy is so darling!"

"I've never seen an ugly puppy," her dad said with a chuckle. "And if they are raised right, there should never be an ugly dog, either. If an animal's personality is lovable, they are lovable, no matter how they look."

"I thought Dalmatians were spotted," Binky said. "This one is almost all white."

"They are born white," Dr. Leighton explained. "This is a very young pup."

He turned to the young couple who owned the puppy. "And remember, this little guy will need your company. Dalmatians need lots of attention and interaction or they can become depressed. Also, they have very good memories and will remember any bad treatment they receive."

"They're a lot like humans!" Jennifer blurted. Everyone laughed.

"Anything living needs to be treated with respect and dignity," Dr. Leighton said. "It's a good lesson to remember."

They departed after a tour of the clinic, with promises from Dr. Leighton that Dmitri could come back and spend an afternoon with him when he was treating patients.

"You must like animals," Jennifer said.

"Very much. I don't have a pet of my own, but I would like one. It seems in America that pets are very popular."

"Especially at our house," Lexi said with a

laugh. Then she told him about her brother Ben's dog and rabbit. "I don't think it will be long before Ben talks Mom and Dad into something else to add to the menagerie."

They drove by the Academy for the Handicapped, where Ben went to school, and then stopped at Mike's garage to say hi to Todd's brother.

"Well, Dmitri, how does this compare to Athens?" Egg asked.

"It is very different," Dmitri said slowly. "Partly because my city and country are very old. The oldest part of Athens was built several hundred years before the birth of Christ."

"And the city isn't all worn out yet?" Binky asked innocently.

Dmitri burst out laughing. "Actually, some of Athens *might* look 'worn out' to you. The ancient city was built around the Acropolis, which is a flat-topped hill. Acropolis means 'upper city.' It is the highest part of the city. Large, beautiful temples were built there to honor the goddess Athena. Today only the ruins of those temples are left. Wars, invasions, visitors, and air pollution have been very hard on those temples, but they are still beautiful. It is exciting to imagine what the Acropolis must have looked like at the time of Christ, since even the ruins are so magnificent."

"We have a statue in the park that's about a hundred years old. I guess that won't impress you much," Jennifer mused.

"Tell us more," Binky urged.

"Many of your words came from our language— democracy, for one."

"Where did they—the Ancient Greeks—shop?" Binky asked.

"Don't you dare ask him if they had malls," Egg warned.

"They did, sort of," Dmitri said, much to everyone's surprise. "At the foot of the Acropolis is the ancient Agora. The Agora was the marketplace. There were meeting spots, shops, and even government offices located there."

"Cool! And it's still all there?"

"Bits and pieces. Of course, Athens also has many skyscrapers. There are apartments and office buildings always growing up around the ruins. The very old and very new are well mixed in Greece. A perfect example is to look up at the Acropolis lit at night and see neon signs advertising products."

"Weird," Binky mused. "Then this place must be very different from your home."

Dmitri looked wistful. "In many ways, yes. Already I am lonely for the sea. There are many beaches where we swim and water-ski. Sometimes we go all the way to Sounion, where there are the ruins of a great old temple that look over the gulf."

"What else do you do?" Jennifer asked. "Where do you hang out? You *do* 'hang out' in Greece, don't you?"

"There are many places in Athens to meet. People come both day and night to sit at tables and visit with family and friends. We eat ices and cakes and drink coffee. Later, when the *tavernas* open, people can have their evening meals and dance. Sometimes we go to the Plaka—the oldest part of the city—which sits in the shadow of the Acropolis. It is always like a party there."

"We must seem pretty dull here in comparison," Egg observed. "And I guess we are."

"Not dull. Just different."

"Let's drive Dmitri to one of the nearby towns," Lexi suggested. "Something smaller than Cedar River. He said there are thousands of tiny towns in Greece. Let's show him one of ours."

Todd glanced at his watch. "Tomorrow is Saturday. I'll start picking everyone up at ten. We'll go on a road trip!"

Jennifer caught Lexi as the group was breaking up. "Wait up. I'd like to talk to you."

Lexi looked at her friend inquisitively.

Jennifer flushed a little and shifted uncomfortably. "I was just wondering what you thought of Dmitri."

"He's great. I could listen to him talk about his country all day. Couldn't you?"

"I could *watch* him talk all day, I know that. He's the best-looking guy I've ever seen."

"Jennifer, you're *blushing*!"

"Lexi, do you think Dmitri could like me?"

"I'm sure he already does."

"No, not like that. I mean really *like* me."

"So you like him?"

"How can I help it? He's cute, funny, smart, exotic. . . ."

"I'll take that as a yes. But I can't tell you more than that."

Jennifer gave a big, gusty sigh. "I just hope nobody else feels about him the way I do. I don't like competition."

Lexi had a sinking feeling in her stomach. She had a hunch there would be *plenty* of competition over a guy like Dmitri.

———

Todd and Dmitri were at Lexi's by 10:15, driving Mrs. Winston's van. Binky, Egg, and Jennifer were with him, too. In fact, Egg was already eating out of the picnic basket Binky had brought along.

"Aren't we going to eat at a restaurant?" Lexi asked as she climbed in. "I didn't bring lunch."

"This is just for the trip. Do you want a banana or a candy bar?"

"We'll be in the car less than an hour!"

"I know. Chips?" Egg was happily scrabbling through the basket. "Good job, Bink. I see you even brought peanuts."

"This is going to be a long trip," Jennifer groaned.

"Longer than you think. Look who's flagging us down." Todd slowed the van. Minda was on the sidewalk, waving frantically.

"Now what?" Jennifer said suspiciously. "She never wants to talk to us."

"Have you forgotten who is in the front seat?" Lexi asked, tilting her head toward Dmitri.

"Oh . . . now things are falling into place."

"Where are you going?" Minda practically fell through Todd's lowered window in her eagerness.

"We're going to show Dmitri around. We're driving out into the country."

"Cool! Can I come?"

Todd's jaw dropped. Egg quit digging in the picnic basket. Binky stared.

"With *us*?" Jennifer was the first to speak.

"Sure. Tressa and Gina are busy this morning. So is Rita. I saw you driving down the street and figured you must be doing something fun."

Silence filled the van. Dmitri looked confused at the cold response Minda was getting. Then Lexi spoke.

"It's fine with me if you come along, Minda. There's plenty of room in the van."

"Sure. It's okay. Hop in," Todd added.

Dmitri smiled, blissfully unaware of the usual hostility between Minda and the others.

"Great." Minda ran to the passenger side of the van and opened the sliding door. "This will be fun," she said as she settled beside Binky.

"Loads," Binky muttered under her breath.

———

"I'm hungry!" Egg announced at five minutes to twelve. "Sight-seeing is very stressful work. Let's stop somewhere to eat."

"Where do you put all that food?" Minda asked incredulously. She'd been amazingly subdued and pleasant as they had been driving.

"I'm a growing boy. Mom says I need to gain weight."

"I'd like your metabolism," Minda said. "Eat and lose weight. Wow."

"There's a place!" Egg pointed at a small diner with the sign "Good Eats" posted outside.

The place was small but clean and smelled

wonderful. While Minda was negotiating a seat next to Dmitri, the other girls escaped to the rest room.

"Can you believe Minda? Crashing our party like that?" Jennifer stewed.

"Actually, she's behaving pretty well," Lexi said charitably.

"Never mind Minda," Binky added. "How about Dmitri? Isn't he gorgeous?"

"He's so sweet," Jennifer mooned. "I think I'm in love."

At that moment, the door flew open and Minda walked in. "Talking about me?" she inquired.

"Hardly. Dmitri."

Minda's expression softened. "He has the most incredible eyes. . . ."

"And smile . . ."

"And—"

"Break it up," Lexi ordered, "before you all melt into a puddle right here in the rest room. The guys are going to wonder what happened to us."

"We ordered for you," Todd said when they returned to the table. "Today's special. Chicken sandwich, fries, and soup."

"I can't eat that!" Minda protested. "Too much fat."

"Dmitri's going to have it," Todd said slyly and watched Minda react.

"What do you eat at home?" Minda asked.

"Seafood is very popular. Personally, I like calimari."

"What's that?" Binky asked.

"Squid."

"With all those legs? Gross!"

"My family also enjoys octopus. We eat stuffed grape leaves and many vegetables. My mother serves a salad with every meal."

"I guess chicken with fries doesn't sound too bad after all," Minda said. "At least it's recognizable to me."

Still, she was picking at her food when the others had finished. There was a brief moment of silence around the table. Then Jennifer startled them all with a blunt question.

"Do you have a girlfriend back home?"

Dmitri considered the question. "Not really. I have many friends who are girls, but there is no one special right now."

"Great! I mean . . ." Minda flushed with embarrassment at her outburst. "Never mind."

Ever the gentleman, Dmitri ignored Minda's faux pas. "My parents don't wish me to become serious about a young woman yet. They do not encourage . . . how do you say it? Romance." He was struggling for the right words to express what he meant, and he sounded very stiff and proper. "They both grew up in small villages and still believe the way their parents did."

"What way is that?" Todd asked.

"First I must explain a little about the villages," Dmitri began. "You have to understand that the people in a village are very loyal to each other. It is much like a family—a very traditional family.

"The villagers are friendly. If you are a traveler who needs help, they will find someone who speaks English to assist you. If there is no taverna at which you can eat, a family will invite you into their home for dinner. People meet in the village square to drink coffee and talk about the news."

"It sounds like a nice place," Binky said. "Cozy."

"It is. Family and community are very important to us. Whole villages celebrate when someone is married. There is a big party with singing and dancing."

"But what does that have to do with you not having a girlfriend?" Egg asked.

"There is a tradition in the villages called *volta*. This means to walk or stroll. On Sundays, the villagers go for a stroll. Young girls walk together as do the young men. Both are in groups. Although they may laugh or smile or wave, boys and girls do not date until they are engaged. In a village, we know each other as family first. Romance comes later."

"What?" Minda nearly screamed the question.

"It's hard for a young American to imagine, I know, but that is how my parents grew up and their parents before them. That is why they don't encourage me to have a girlfriend. Even though they understand that times are changing, they remember how it was for them."

"That is totally weird!" Minda proclaimed. "I wouldn't want to live in a village like that."

"Oh, but they are very beautiful one-story whitewashed houses with red tile roofs. Inside, people decorate with hand-made pottery and cloth. It is a warm and friendly place."

"So even though you could date, you don't do it

much because your parents are uncomfortable with it?" Lexi summarized.

"Yes."

"But now you're in America," Jennifer pointed out. "Is that going to make a difference?"

Dmitri looked from Jennifer to Minda and back again. "My parents told me that while I am here, I must learn American customs."

Binky squealed. "I think he just said yes!"

———————

"Lexi, Jennifer, come inside so I can show you my computer," Binky invited when Todd drove into the McNaughtons' driveway. Minda had been the first to be dropped off. "Please?" she pleaded. "I need help—big time."

"Binky, we aren't that computer literate," Jennifer said as they followed her to the house. Egg loped ahead, carrying the now-empty picnic basket.

"You can do e-mail, can't you? All I need help for is to hook up my modem, set up some Internet access software, log on, and go on-line."

"Get a grip on reality, Binky. You need more help than we can give you," Jennifer replied.

"You've had computer classes."

"So has Egg."

"Egg is less than no help at all," Binky retorted shortly. "All he does is moan and groan and offer dumb advice and food."

They were standing in front of the McNaughton computer. It was perched on a desk piled high with how-to books for computers and their operators. Cookies spilled out of a foil bag on one side, and soda cans cluttered the other. A pile of candy wrappers and empty jars littered the floor around the chair.

"Egg, get that old sandwich off the seat! I want to sit down. Lexi and Jennifer are going to help me get on the World Wide Web. Now where's that 'on' switch again?"

The two girls stared at each other in horror. *That's* what Binky was expecting?

"Sorry, Bink. Gotta go," Jennifer said. "We'd be old women before we could help you that much."

"Me too," Lexi added. Mentally she was thinking, *Because we don't have all night*.

"You guys are no fun," Binky grumbled. "So I'll do it myself. I can read. Therefore, I can figure this out." She punched a few keys, and words and icons flitted across the screen. "But before you go, just tell me what the words 'Program Deleted' really mean."

Chapter Three

Mrs. Waverly was particularly excited about Dmitri's presence in school. She had been to Greece twice and was delighted to find someone who shared her enthusiasm for the lovely islands. She stopped Dmitri as he entered the music room for chorus.

"I'm so happy you are here," she said sincerely. "You have a very beautiful homeland."

Dmitri's dark eyes twinkled. "Thank you. I agree."

"It must have been hard to leave it," Mrs. Waverly observed.

"In many ways, yes, but it is interesting here, too." He waved a hand across the filling room, indicating the students who were all listening. "I'm very busy learning new customs."

Mrs. Waverly beamed. "The Greek people are the friendliest I've ever met in my travels. Several times while I was in Greece I was invited into the homes of the locals. Here in America, we've lost that kind of hospitality."

"You mean they just invited you inside without knowing who you were?" Tressa asked.

"Yes, they are always very willing to make coffee for a guest or offer you some sort of drink." Mrs. Waverly smiled at the remembrance. "I always thought it was interesting that I was given a bit of jam and a teaspoon served on the rim of a glass of cold water as a sign of their hospitality."

"What did you do with it?" Binky asked.

"Well, first I ate the jam. Then I put the empty spoon in the glass of water."

"You mean you had to wash your own dish?"

"Not exactly. Then I drank the water."

Binky looked as if she thought the ritual rather bizarre.

Mrs. Waverly laughed. "Sometimes I was served a cup of coffee. It's very different from the coffee we drink in America. The cup is tiny. The coffee is very strong and usually sweetened."

"Well, what do you do with that?" Egg was getting interested.

"Just sip it slowly. One cup is plenty because it is very strong and thick. Usually there is sediment in the bottom of the cup, which, of course, you don't drink.

"One of the most exciting times in my life," Mrs. Waverly continued, "was visiting Greece and having the privilege of meeting school teachers from that country."

"So you have friends in Greece?" Dmitri asked eagerly.

"Only one now. We exchange letters once or twice a year. She teaches elementary school, primarily reading and writing. She told me that teaching the reading and writing of Greek is not an easy task. For nearly a century and a half there were two Greek languages, Dimotiki and Katharevousa. The second language was never spoken in Greece but was taught anyway because many books and documents were written in it. My friend was very relived when in 1975 that language was dropped from the curriculum."

"It's weird to look at," Binky pointed out, referring to the Greek letters on Dmitri's shirt.

Dmitri laughed. "It looks very familiar and comfortable to me. To me English and your alphabet is sometimes confusing."

"Does your friend still teach school, Mrs. Waverly?" Lexi asked.

"Yes, she does. But she's near retirement age now. She will be sorry to quit teaching. She says that although there are still not enough schools and enough space for students, books and education have improved a great deal in Greece in the past few years."

Dmitri nodded. "That is what my parents say also. They find education very important. That is why they allowed me to come to the United States of America to study. They thought it would be good for my mind."

"I know going to Greece would be good for mine," Binky said. "The sun, the sea, the sand . . ."

"That sounds fine to me." Tim Anders walked by and caught the last part of Binky's statement. "What are you describing?"

"Dmitri can tell you all about it in class," Mrs. Waverly said to Tim.

The others looked at her in surprise.

"He can?"

"Yes. I've already found some Greek folk songs that I thought might be fun to try in chorus today. But since there is so much interest in Dmitri's country, and it will make the songs so much more meaningful if we know a little more about the land in which he lives. We'll devote today to learning about Greece. Then tomorrow we can learn the songs."

"Cool. You mean we don't have to sing today?" Tressa Williams always liked it when a teacher changed plans for a class. If Mr. Drummond had announced that instead of studying history in his class, they were going to sing, that would have made her happy, too.

"Dmitri, would you be willing to share with us some things about Greece?" Mrs. Waverly asked.

Dmitri looked shy and pleased at the same time. "It would be my honor to do that for you," he said in the stiff, proper way he often spoke.

Out of the corner of her eye, Lexi could see Minda and Gina staring at him with love-sick expressions.

"Take your seats, please," Mrs. Waverly commanded. Then she explained to the entire chorus about her plan for the Greek songs and spending the day learning more about the country they came from.

Dmitri, surprisingly calm and poised, took his place beside her behind a music stand. "Thank you." His dark eyes twinkled as he shifted from foot to foot. It was the only sign he gave that he was nervous.

"I like to talk about my country. We Greeks are very proud of our country because it is old and has been the birthplace of many wonderful things, such as democracy and the Olympics. That is especially exciting here because you have read about my home in your history books. In Greece, we students must go to school for nine years. We go to elementary school until we are fifteen years old. Then we may attend a secondary school that prepares us for the university or vocational training. Greek students must work very hard in school and take examinations. Teachers, and education itself, are considered very important in Greece. Our schooling is free from kindergarten through the university. Even the textbooks are given to us."

"Wow! That's a deal," Gina piped. "You don't have to pay for any of it?"

"No, but we're expected to do very well. There is much studying involved," Dmitri said.

"No parties, huh?" Gina grinned.

Dmitri smiled. "Only if they don't interfere with your studying."

Lexi saw Minda yawn. She had a hunch Minda was glad she wasn't going to school in Greece.

"Why don't you tell us a little bit about how the people in Greece earn their living?" Mrs. Waverly encouraged.

"Even though Greece is mountainous, very rocky, and much of the land can't be cultivated, agriculture is one of our chief sources of income. The farms are small by American standards. Eight to ten acres is considered average. Even so, Greek farmers have to work hard to make any sort of living from the land. Often the whole family must work outside in the fields or with the animals.

"We raise tobacco, wheat, olives, citrus fruits, apples, and peaches," Dmitri continued. "Wine, olive oil, and raisins are also very important to our economy. We follow the traditions of the ancient days in another way. Greece has many shipbuilders and many shipping businesses. Athens' seaport, Piraeus, is the most active and the most important." Smile lines crinkled around Dmitri's eyes. "I love to go to the port of Piraeus and watch the people," he admitted.

"Huge cruise ships carrying tourists from all over the world come there, docking and embarking on tours around our seas. Car ferries and tankers come and go, as well. There are many fishermen in Greece and a great number of factories. Because Greece has so many beautiful places and so many historic sites, tourism has become an important source of income."

"What's there to see?" Tressa asked.

Dmitri's eyes flew open in surprise. "There are many things: the Acropolis and all the other ruins; the places that Saint Paul visited when he was in Greece; and, of course, the mountains and beaches. But even better are its people," Dmitri said with a smile.

"What do your parents do?" Lexi asked.

A proud look came into Dmitri's eyes. "My mother owns her own business. A souvenir shop for the tourists. She sells clothing and trinkets as well as some very fine glassware." Dmitri plucked at his shirt. It was white with full sleeves and a small collar. "This came from my mother's shop," he said.

"And what about your dad?" Egg asked.

"My father drives a taxi," Dmitri said. "It is a very important occupation in Greece. He owns his own vehicle and keeps it very clean." Dmitri grinned and looked around the room. "It is a Mercedes Benz."

The boys whistled low under their breaths. "Nice car."

Dmitri nodded. "Yes, it is durable and reliable. Sometimes when my father has tourists in the car, he stops to show them my mother's souvenir store. It is a very handy system. My mother serves his passengers beverages and asks them to look around her shop.

"My uncle and my grandfather farm in a small village just outside of Athens. It is where my father and mother grew up. Athens has grown so much that the small village in which they live is on the border of the city now, but at one time it was far out in the country, away from all the people in town. My mother inherited her shop from her uncle, who sold mainly fruits and breads there."

"Do you have any other family?" Binky asked. The entire room was very quiet. Everyone was obviously interested in Dmitri's story.

"I have an older sister who is married and has three children, but they live on the island of Santorini because her husband is a jewelry maker.

That means I don't get to see them as often as I would like, although it is not very difficult to go by boat between the islands."

"America must seem very boring to you after an exciting place like Greece," Minda commented. As she spoke, she looked up through her eyelashes at Dmitri. Then she batted them coyly—a "majorly flirtatious move," as Gina or Tressa might say. Minda was publicly staking her claim on Dmitri.

"Oh no. It is very exciting," Dmitri said, unaffected by Minda's behavior. "You, too, have a democratic government and a very fine and beautiful country."

"Well, I never thought about it that way," Minda said.

"Then that's a good point to end on today," Mrs. Waverly said. "It's good that we learn to appreciate our own home."

"But we have more questions to ask," Gina protested.

Mrs. Waverly pointed at the clock. "The bell is about to ring. We are out of time for today."

"Already?" Everyone was surprised at how quickly the hour had flown by.

"Tomorrow we are going to sing Greek folk songs. One or two may be familiar, but most won't, so plan to learn some new music."

Tressa and Gina groaned at that announcement, but no one else seemed to mind. A small group followed Dmitri out the door, darting him with questions.

As the guys disappeared into the gym, Lexi,

Peggy, Binky, Angela, and Jennifer gathered at their lockers.

"It was interesting to hear what Dmitri told us about his country," Jennifer said.

"I agree," Peggy responded. "I could listen to him all day."

"So could Minda Hannaford," Jennifer said with a grimace. "She was acting so attentive that if she'd sat any straighter, her head might have snapped right off her body."

"Give her a break, Jennifer," Lexi advised. "Maybe she was actually interested. It was pretty fascinating stuff he was saying, you know."

Jennifer snorted. "Minda interested in information just for the sake of information? I don't think so."

Binky appeared totally unaware of the conversation the girls were having. She was muttering to herself and digging in her locker. "I know I put that book in here somewhere. I had it in my hand this morning. Don't tell me I left it on the table at home. I can't have left it there!"

"What's your problem, Binky?" Peggy asked with a sigh.

"I need to study the computer book I bought," Binky said. "I've got a book that defines all those stupid little icons. Why can't computers just use words? Isn't that what computers are about, anyway—words? I can't tell the little files from the little printer, and I haven't got a clue what some of the other things mean."

"Why is it so important right now?" Lexi asked.

"Because I want to learn how to send e-mail, of

course." Binky looked at her friend in disbelief. "After hearing what Dmitri had to say, can you blame me? He's so cool and he had so much interesting information. I want to talk to somebody in a foreign country, and I could do it if I had e-mail. I have to find someone who can help me. Jennifer, do you have any suggestions?"

Jennifer shrugged helplessly. She'd avoided computer classes because of her dyslexia. It wasn't apparent what Binky's excuse was.

Lexi noticed that Angela Hardy had come up to the lockers, too. She had a sad, faraway look on her face.

"Hi, Angela. How are you?"

"Okay."

The short answer was not characteristic of Angela.

"Is everything all right?" Lexi asked with concern in her voice.

"Fine."

Lexi knew immediately that Angela was anything but fine.

"I haven't talked to you for a while," she said to Angela. "Are you doing anything special after school? Do you want to come over to my house? We can find something to eat and listen to music."

Angela hesitated at first and then shrugged. "Sure, why not."

"Good. I'll meet you here after school."

———

Angela had very little to say on the way to the Leightons' home. Lexi was thankful for the people who greeted them or stopped to talk. Angela's silence was growing uncomfortable. Fortunately, both Lexi's mother and younger brother were home when they arrived, and their house was full of activity. Ben and Wiggles, Ben's puppy, were doing somersaults across the living-room floor. Mrs. Leighton, wearing a paint-spattered smock, sat in one of the chairs, clapping as her son and his pet tumbled around the room.

Ben, who had Down's syndrome, had some trouble with coordination, but it was not apparent today as he and Wiggles careened about the room like acrobats.

"Hello, girls," Mrs. Leighton greeted the pair as they entered. "Angela, it's nice to see you. You haven't been here for a while."

"No, ma'am, I guess I've been busy."

"How's your mother?" Mrs. Leighton asked.

A spark of emotion flashed in Angela's eyes, and her lips tightened. "Fine" was all she said.

"I have had the best day today," Mrs. Leighton told Lexi, seeming not to notice Angela's odd response. "I finished three paintings I've been meaning to get to for weeks. They all just needed a touch here or there, but I couldn't seem to motivate myself to do it."

"You must be feeling better," Lexi pointed out.

"Exceptionally good today. That's what is so strange about MS. It's a very unpredictable disease, but I want to take advantage of my good days." Mrs. Leighton stood up. "So I think I will try to finish one more painting. Then I can make a trip to the frame shop that won't be time wasted."

"Remember, the doctor said not to overdo," Lexi reminded her mother.

"Don't worry, this isn't hard. Frankly, I'm enjoying the feeling of making progress for a change. There's food in the fridge if you girls are hungry. Ben, make sure you don't get Wiggles too excited. And put him back on his chain in the yard when you're done playing."

"Okay," Ben said from his upside-down position on the carpet. Wiggles was cheerfully licking his face.

"It's nice to see my mother like that," Lexi said after Mrs. Leighton had disappeared into her studio. "She doesn't always feel very well. We all enjoy the days she's feeling good."

"You're lucky," Angela said wistfully.

"Because my mom's feeling better? I think so, too."

"No, because you have such a great mom," Angela corrected.

"Well, I know I'm lucky for that, but you're lucky, too. Your mother is amazing."

"Amazing? Yeah, right." Angela's tone was sarcastic.

"No, I mean it. Think about it, Angela. You and your mom were homeless, and now you have an apartment, she has a job, and you both have brand-new lives. What your mother has accomplished for the two of you really *is* amazing. You might not appreciate it because you're too close to the situation, but it's true."

Angela shook her head. "It's not that," she

blurted. "It's not about us no longer being home-less."

"Then what is this about?" Lexi asked. "You've looked sad all day."

"I really can't say anything," Angela mur-mured.

"It won't go any farther than this room. I prom-ise," Lexi assured her.

Angela glanced down at the floor and took a deep breath. "My mom has started dating some-one."

"Really? That's great! I'll bet she's having a fun time."

Angela looked disconcerted, then doubtful. "I don't know about that. All I know is that I don't like him."

"What's wrong with him?" Lexi asked.

"I can't really explain it," Angela said slowly. "Just something inside that makes me uneasy."

"Does he say things to you or do things that you don't like?"

"No, he's very polite and he never does any-thing that he shouldn't. It's just that . . ." She screwed up her face in confusion. "He's changed my mom."

"Changed her? Does he make her do things she doesn't want to do?"

"No, of course not. Nothing like that. It's just that she's gotten so silly about him."

"Oh," Lexi nodded knowingly. "Like she might be in love with him or something?"

"No, she'd never love him," Angela protested too

much. "But he's changed the way my mom feels about me."

Lexi stared at her friend. "What do you mean by that?"

"She just doesn't have time for me like she used to," Angela admitted. "This man is all she thinks about, and sometimes he even acts like I don't exist. My mother is behaving like a love-sick teenager. Can you believe it? Isn't that gross?"

"Oh, that doesn't sound so bad, unless she begins acting like Binky when she talks about Harry. She does get pretty crazy sometimes."

"I shouldn't have used that example. This is totally different," Angela said, her expression so serious that frown lines marred her forehead. "My mom is jumping into this dating thing way too fast. She's been asked out in the past and she's dated, but it never led to anything. This guy asks her out to dinner two or three nights a week."

"Well, that sounds nice," Lexi said.

"Maybe it does if it's not your mother he's asking out. I'm not crazy about eating at home alone, you know." Angela crossed her arms over her chest and stared at the ground.

Something niggled in the back of Lexi's mind. *Could it be that Angela is jealous?* It sounded that way. On the other hand, Angela knew her mother very well. Maybe this man wasn't right for her, and Angela was just unable to pinpoint how or why or put it into words.

"Just forget I said it. Forget all about it. I don't want to talk about this anymore. If my mom is going to mess up her life, I should just let her do it. She's a big girl now."

Lexi would have protested, but Angela changed the subject. "Show me the new outfit you've been making. I would love to see it."

"Well, I suppose." Lexi started for the staircase. "It's in my room."

The girls climbed the steps to Lexi's bedroom, discussing clothing designs and outfits. It was as if Angela felt she had said too much and was now refusing to say anything more.

Lexi, who could talk about her hobby of sewing all day long, became engrossed with the details of her latest project. The earlier conversation between the two girls was forgotten.

Chapter Four

"Are you planning to study with us?" Lexi asked Todd and Egg as they passed her in the hall. Peggy, Binky, and Jennifer were waiting nearby holding their books. "And Dmitri, too, of course."

"Not today," Todd said. "We're going running."

"Can't you tell?" Egg sounded indignant. He was wearing shorts, which revealed his scrawny white legs above thick athletic socks and tennis shoes.

"No, we thought you always dressed that way," Binky retorted to her brother. "Frankly, all I can tell is that you look pretty funny. And, by the way, why are you going running? I thought you didn't like exercise."

Egg gave his sister a disparaging look. "I love exercise. I just don't do enough of it, but Dmitri has to get in shape."

Jennifer eyed the dark-haired guy from head to toe and came up with her own conclusion. "He looks like he's in great shape to me."

Was it possible? Had Jennifer actually winked at Dmitri? Or had Lexi just imagined that slight lifting of the shoulder, the shy smile? Was Jennifer *flirting*?

But before Lexi could digest this bit of information, Jennifer added, "But *you* could use a little work, Egg."

Before Egg could bluster a response, Todd broke into the conversation. "Dmitri is very active in sports in Greece," he explained. "He's planning to run in our next track meet."

"Sports have been a major part of Greece's culture for nearly three thousand years," Peggy said proudly. "Isn't that right, Dmitri?"

"That's right. A foot race was the first contest," he said. "The Greek city-states all sent their best athletes to run, and the winner was crowned with a garland of olive leaves and was known as a hero. Later, we added wrestling, chariot races, and discus throwing. Of course, like so many things, even the Olympic games became corrupt and were finally abolished."

"Just recently?" Binky asked innocently.

Dmitri laughed. "No, in about the year 394 A.D."

"Oh." Binky's face turned bright pink.

"The Olympic games were resurrected in 1896," Dmitri was quick to explain. "Our people have always loved sports. We play soccer and football, basketball and volleyball, and, of course, we love water sports like swimming, sailing, and diving. Athens also has both tennis courts and golf courses."

"I guess I should have listened better in class," Binky murmured, more to herself than to the others.

"Actually, in ancient times, Greece had a very good idea," Dmitri continued. "All wars were stopped as long as the games were being played.

That way the entire country's attention would be turned to the Olympics and not divided."

"Cool. I wish we had something that could manage that," Peggy said.

"I hate to break up this interesting conversation," Todd interrupted, "but we have to get going if we're going to get several miles in today."

Egg looked wearily at Todd. "Several *miles*? You never said anything before about several *miles*."

Covering her mouth with her hands, Lexi turned away to hide her smile. "Since the guys sound like they are going to be very busy, why don't we go to the Hamburger Shack?"

"Fine with me," Peggy answered.

"Me too," said Binky.

"Let's ask Angela and Anna Marie if they want to go along," Jennifer suggested.

As they walked away from the guys, Egg was still complaining about having to run farther than he'd planned.

———

Jerry Randall greeted them at the door of the Hamburger Shack. "What is this? Girls' night out? Where are Todd and Egg?"

"Running," Binky said.

"Todd I can believe, but Egg. . . ?"

"It's a long story," Lexi said. "I'm sure Egg will tell you all about it tomorrow when he comes wobbling in here hardly able to walk."

"What do you mean by girls' night out?" Jennifer asked.

Jerry tilted his head toward a table at the other

side of the room. The Hi-Fives were in their usual spot, talking and giggling.

"You don't think we came to see them, do you?" Binky asked, insulted.

"I thought you had something in common."

"What's that?" Peggy said.

"Dmitri. Isn't every girl in school crazy about him? He's all those girls have talked about since they arrived."

"Thanks for the warning." Jennifer led them to the table she and her friends usually occupied. From where they sat, they could hear Minda, Tressa, Gina, and Rita talking.

"He's so incredibly handsome. Those eyes. That dark hair. I like the color of his skin, don't you? It's kind of an olive-tan color, like he's been in the sun his whole life. Like a lifeguard or something."

"Oh brother," Jennifer muttered under her breath.

"Shhh," Binky said. "Be quiet. I'm trying to listen."

"I like his accent," Gina said. "It's so foreign."

"That's because he *is* foreign, silly," Peggy muttered under her breath.

"I like the way he walks," Rita said bluntly. "Men who are athletic looking are cool."

"Huh," Binky said. "You just like men in general. Rita, you are so boy crazy. . . ."

"Shhh." Everyone at Binky's table turned to her, glaring at her to be quiet.

The Hi-Fives were trying to outdo one another with praise for Dmitri, while Minda sat at the head of the table, looking smug. Finally, she spoke.

"Well, I'm so glad you girls all like Dmitri. That means you approve of my next boyfriend."

"You and Dmitri? Do you really think so?" Gina looked impressed.

Binky rolled her eyes and started to giggle.

"Binky, please be quiet. Minda is going to hear you," Lexi whispered. "We're not supposed to be eavesdropping on their conversation."

"They're practically yelling, Lexi. It's not like we have to lean our ears up against a door to hear what they're saying."

"Actually, I don't want to hear it at all." Jennifer stood up, and the chair skidded away from the table as the back of her legs hit it. "I don't have to listen to this garbage. I'm going home. Anybody who wants to can come with me. I'll make root beer floats." She turned and walked toward the door.

The other girls gathered up their things and followed her.

"Guess who has her own crush on Dmitri," Binky chortled as they left the Hamburger Shack.

Jennifer turned to glare at her, but she didn't say anything.

———

Lexi and Jennifer were the last to join the gang in the school lunchroom the next afternoon. Everyone was laughing at Dmitri as he moved his food around on the plate with a dismayed expression on his face.

"What's wrong?" Jennifer slid her tray onto the table and reached for the ketchup. "It's chicken nuggets and fries. One of my favorite meals."

Dmitri's dark eyes grew wide. "It is? You *like* this?" He poked at the congealed fat that lay beneath his now cold chicken nuggets. "And these?" He held up a limp French fry that drooped between his fingers.

"Well, you let it get cold," Jennifer pointed out. "They're much better hot."

"Nothing comes out of this cafeteria hot," Egg reminded her.

"Well, that's true, but at least a little bit warm is better than ice-cold. Have you even tried it?"

Dmitri nodded mournfully. "But I did not recognize it . . . as food, I mean."

"He's being pretty hard on your favorite meal," Matt teased.

Jennifer speared a chicken nugget with gusto. "I don't care; I like this stuff. Junk food is my friend."

Dmitri looked at her sadly. "You wouldn't say that if you could taste the food we have in Greece."

"You mean you don't like any American food?" Jennifer asked.

"I like the food Todd's mother cooks." Dmitri brightened. "Meatballs and mashed potatoes, steak, baked beans, coleslaw, and strawberry pie. They're all very good."

"Well, I like those foods, too," Jennifer assured him. "But what about junk food? Fast food?"

"Much of it does not have a taste," Dmitri said. "I like my food with many spices, and I like food cooked in olive oil, not in whatever this is." He pointed to the puddle of grease. "Many of the foods we eat in Greece are fresh. My mother shops at the market every day. We have fresh caught fish from the sea, vegetables from the garden, and delicious salads made with goat cheese and tomatoes. They are very fine. My mother also makes wonderful desserts with filo dough and ground nuts and honey." Dmitri closed his eyes, and a smile lurked on the corners of his lips as if he was remembering his mother's meals. "It is wonderful."

"Goat cheese," Egg said in horror. "Excuse me. You like eating goat cheese? That sounds awful."

"And I don't like olives," Matt said. "Greeks eat a lot of olives, don't they?"

Dmitri put his hands palms down on the tabletop. A determined expression settled across his features. "You don't believe me? Then I will cook you a real Greek meal and show you what it's like. You Americans don't even know what you are missing."

"You'd cook for us?" Lexi gasped.

"What a great idea," Jennifer said.

"But where would you get the ingredients?" Matt wondered.

"My mother could help him find them," Todd said. "We can do it at my house. Mom and Dad will think it's an excellent idea, too."

"Lexi and I could help you do the grocery shopping, Dmitri," Jennifer offered.

Lexi looked startled. That thought hadn't occurred to her.

"Good. Then we wouldn't have to trouble Mrs. Winston about that," Dmitri said. "When shall I cook this meal?"

"How about Saturday night?" Todd suggested. "Jennifer and Lexi could help you shop Saturday morning. Mom will be around all day if you need help with anything."

"It is settled, then. On Saturday night you will begin to understand how wonderful Greek food can be."

"This is going to be fun," Binky chimed.

"With goat cheese . . ." Egg said suspiciously. "We'll just have to wait and see."

Chapter Five

Todd answered the door on Saturday morning, barefoot and his hair tousled. He scratched his head and peered at the girls in the doorway through squinted eyes.

"Did you just get up?" Jennifer asked as she stepped inside. "I thought we were supposed to pick Dmitri up before nine."

"He's eating breakfast. He didn't wake me up this morning. Guess he let me sleep in so I'll be ready to do some serious cooking this afternoon. Besides, I didn't know you got up before noon on Saturdays, Jennifer."

"Very funny."

Todd was spared any more comments as Dmitri entered the room. He was considerably more alert than Todd. He wore dark jeans, a navy-and-white-striped shirt, and he carried a large sheet of paper in his hands.

"Are you ready to shop?" Lexi asked.

"I don't know if he's ready for this," Todd said doubtfully. "Dmitri, do you have any idea what it might be like shopping with these two?"

"I have shopped in the open markets of Athens.

Can it be more difficult than that?" Dmitri turned to Todd. "Does your mother have a wooden spoon in her kitchen?"

Todd looked blank. "I don't know. Why?"

"I cannot cook without a wooden spoon. It is the Greek way."

The Greek way. They knew they were going to hear that a lot before Dmitri's meal was done.

———————

"How is shopping in Greece different from this?" Jennifer asked.

They were standing in the shopping cart corral of Cedar River's largest grocery store. There were fresh flowers on display near the produce, magazines and videos were being sold on long racks, and a pharmacist was dispensing medication from behind a counter along the wall.

"Where is the food?" Dmitri exclaimed.

Lexi and Jennifer burst into laughter. Lexi took a cart and began to push it past the flowers. "This way."

"Shopping will be much faster here," Dmitri observed. "If I do not get lost."

"Tell us what to look for," Lexi said. "It will go even more quickly with three of us taking a portion of the list."

Dmitri nodded and checked his paper. "Jennifer, will you get two pounds of ground lamb?"

"Ground lamb? I don't think I've ever seen that here. Of course, I've never looked. . . ."

"Ground beef will work. It won't be as authentic, but it will do," Dmitri assured her. "And, Lexi, will you get three eggplants? And lemons—several lemons."

"Lamb and eggplant?" Jennifer hissed as they left Dmitri studying the spices. "There's no way I'm going to eat that stuff!"

"Calm down, Jennifer. It might be great."

By the time they returned with their foods, Dmitri had found several of the items on his list—filo dough, goat cheese, garlic cloves, and walnuts.

"What's this?" Jennifer picked up the cheese.

"Goat cheese," Dmitri said.

The look of dismay on Jennifer's face prompted him to say, "This cheese is a very important part of our diet. The shepherds make it from the milk of their animals. Feta cheese is eaten in the morning on warm bread or toast. It is served with olives, cucumbers, and tomatoes. My mother uses it for salad every day and for cheese pies."

Dmitri looked so concerned that Jennifer would not like the cheese that she said, "I'm sure it's delicious. It's just that I've never had it before, that's all."

"That's why we're having Dmitri cook for us," Lexi interjected. "I'm excited. I think it will be delicious!"

As they followed him up and down the aisles, Jennifer whispered, "Did you really mean it when you said you thought this food would be good?"

"Yes, I did. Quit worrying and be a good sport. I'm sure it will be fine. People in Greece eat like this all the time. It's a great opportunity."

"What's he doing now?"

Dmitri was planted in front of the dairy case with a frown on his face.

"What are you looking for?" Lexi asked.

"Yogurt."

"It's right here." Jennifer pointed to an entire section of flavored yogurt.

"It's full of fruit and flavors!" Dmitri said disdainfully. "What good is that? Yogurt is best plain, don't you think?"

"This is going to be a very interesting meal," Jennifer muttered. "Maybe it won't be edible, but it will be interesting!"

Lexi smiled to herself as she noticed that she kept getting left behind when Dmitri and Jennifer were searching for another item on his list. Dmitri was intent on the perfect ingredients. Jennifer was intent on Dmitri. She looked at him with an admiring expression that told Lexi her friend was falling hard for this handsome Greek.

And Dmitri didn't seem opposed to Jennifer's interest, either. His smile was wide and bright when she spoke to him, and they spent a lot of time laughing together.

"Let's have some cappuccino before we leave," Lexi suggested. She had a hunch neither of them would mind prolonging the shopping trip. "The coffee shop here is excellent."

"This, too, is very different," Dmitri commented as he sipped his espresso and flipped through a magazine. "Many of the shops in Greece are still owned and run by families. Of course, Athens has supermarkets similar to this, but my family, like many others, prefer to buy from the small shops and markets. At the bakery, we can watch what we buy being pulled out of the ovens.

"My mother especially likes the markets where the stalls are full of vegetables and cheeses. We buy bread, olives, sugar, and spices by weight. She usually buys her meat there, too."

"Isn't that unhandy?" Lexi asked. "She must have to do a lot of walking to get her shopping done."

Dmitri laughed and gestured toward the huge expanse of the mega-store. "No more than this. Besides, the market stalls also sell clothes and shoes. *Kiosks* have stamps and paper. She can get everything she needs."

"What are 'kiosks'?" Jennifer asked.

"They are booths on street corners. Some sell magazines or have a public telephone. People often gather around a kiosk just to talk."

"It sounds cozy," Lexi said. "I think I'd like it."

"Then you must come to visit." He turned to Jennifer. "And you, too."

"I think I'll wait to see how I like the food tonight first."

———

Mrs. Winston met them at the front door as they lugged their grocery bags to the house. "You really did shop, didn't you? Can I help with anything?"

"I think we'll make it," Jennifer puffed. "We've got half the store here!"

"I haven't heard yet what Dmitri is planning to

make," Mrs. Winston said as she peered into a bag. "Yum. Eggplant."

"If you say so," Jennifer said doubtfully. "If it tastes like it looks, it's got to be gross."

"We don't know what he's making, either. We didn't ask. But we do know the ingredients!" Lexi said.

Dmitri heard her comment as he carried the last bags into the house.

"My favorites—*mousaka*, Greek salad, *skordalia, tiropites*, and *baklava*."

"How can I eat what I can't even pronounce?" Jennifer muttered.

"How wonderful!" Mrs. Winston exclaimed. "I love Greek food. Here, let me help you unload those groceries."

Todd was in the kitchen taking dishes out of the cupboard. "You're back already? I thought you'd be gone for hours. I was going to set the table for tonight."

"I'll help you," Jennifer offered.

Lexi turned to Dmitri. "What should I do?"

He frowned at the piles of groceries. "I think I should start the mousaka first. Will you peel the eggplant and slice it while I brown the meat?"

"Sure, although I don't think I've ever even *held* an eggplant before today."

"Mousaka is a very traditional Greek food." Dmitri said.

As Dmitri began to explain it, Lexi burst into laughter. "That's what we call a casserole or a hot dish! I guess Greek food isn't so mysterious after all."

While Dmitri assembled the mousaka, Lexi made tiropites—tiny cheese pies—from filo pastry. She placed a cheese mixture into the pastry strips, then folded them into triangles.

Lexi had just finished when Todd and Jennifer returned to the kitchen.

"All done," Todd said. "We'll put out the yogurt, lemons, and olives just before everyone sits down to eat."

"Why?" Jennifer asked. "Is that our only food? After all the groceries we bought?"

"It is the Greek way," Dmitri said simply. "You wanted an *authentic* Greek meal? This will be one."

"Which reminds me, if we don't go home and clean up, we won't get back here in time to eat." Lexi turned to Jennifer. "Let's go."

Todd and Dmitri were slicing cucumbers for salad when Lexi and Jennifer left, promising to be back later to help with some of the cooking—and *all* of the eating.

———

Matt, Angela, Binky, Egg, and Jennifer had already arrived when Peggy and Lexi rang the doorbell.

"Don't you look nice!" Lexi murmured when Egg opened the door. "You're wearing a *suit*!"

"A sport coat, actually. My sister made me do it. You look pretty nice yourself."

"I'm glad you told me to dress up," Peggy said as they entered. She paused, then added, "Wow!"

Candles were burning everywhere in the

house. Wonderful aromas were wafting from the kitchen. Music—Greek, of course—was playing in the background. Mrs. Winston breezed toward them in a shimmery chiffon evening dress, her hair piled high on her head, glittery earrings sparkling on her ears.

"Welcome!"

"This is so cool," Peggy breathed.

"I hope you don't mind us 'old folks' joining the fun," Mrs. Winston said. "But we couldn't resist an authentic Greek meal. Todd's father and I spent three weeks in Greece, and I've never been able to get that beautiful country out of my system."

"I'm glad," Lexi said. "This is too special to miss."

Just then Dmitri burst out of the kitchen, carrying two potholders. "Come!" he demanded. "Everything is ready."

The table was bright with flickering candles.

"Place cards and cloth napkins?" Binky sounded impressed. She looked even *more* impressed when Dmitri pulled out her chair for her. That gentlemanly move inspired the other guys to do the same.

"Mom, will you say the blessing?" Todd asked. "And then Dmitri will say in Greek the grace his family uses."

When the chorus of amens was complete, Egg looked over the table and pointed to a dish that appeared to be a white pudding flecked with green. "This is great, but what is it?"

"*Tzatziki*. It is a favorite in Greece. Dip your

bread in it and eat it as an appetizer."

To everyone's surprise, it was Egg who first took a piece of pita bread and dipped it in the concoction. He chewed and licked his lips. "It's actually good! Really good."

That was all it took. Everyone began to fill up their plates. The next few minutes were taken up with the business of eating and the murmurs of pleasure.

"Where's dessert?" Egg asked after he'd polished off most of what might have been leftovers for tomorrow.

Dmitri jumped to his feet. "I'll get it."

"And I'll help you." Jennifer was just as quick to leap up.

"Should we let them be alone in the kitchen?" Todd asked.

Egg made smooching sounds on the back of his arm.

"Grow up, you two!" Binky ordered. "If Jennifer likes Dmitri, what's it to you?"

"I just hope she doesn't like him too much," Todd said.

"Why?"

"Because Minda likes Dmitri, too. And Minda always gets her way. I just don't want Jennifer to get hurt."

"Stop it," Lexi said. "I don't blame Jennifer for liking him. He's handsome, charming, exotic . . ."

"Should I be jealous?" Todd asked playfully.

"If anybody is going to be jealous, it will be Minda," Binky said calmly. "Am I right?"

"You're all being silly," Peggy said with finality.

"Friendship doesn't have to turn into romance. It can turn into . . . well, *friendship*!"

She was saved from explaining that statement to her friends because the kitchen door flew open as Dmitri carried the dessert to the table.

———

"That was the best meal I've ever eaten!" Peggy proclaimed as they sat around the table, drinking Greek coffee and eating baklava.

"What's in this stuff, anyway?"

"Filo pastry and walnuts, mostly."

Lexi looked down at the diamond-shaped dessert decorated with cloves and soaked in syrup. "There must be a million calories in this, but I don't even care."

"And the coffee is delicious." Mr. Winston lifted his demitasse cup. "But it's not quite like American coffee. You only need one cup."

"If you want to make it again, use a teaspoon of instant coffee, one teaspoon of sugar, and half a cup of water. Bring it to a boil several times." Dmitri put his thumb and forefinger together and touched his lips. "Delicious." Then his face fell. "I only wish I could have found grape leaves in your store so that I could have made *dolmades*."

"Don't feel bad," Egg said, holding his stomach. "I didn't have anyplace to put them."

"And if *he* didn't have anyplace," Binky said, "then no one would. Egg has two hollow legs, you know. He stuffs them first before his stomach even starts to feel full."

"Hey! I don't eat that much."

"Yes, you do. I don't know how he does it," Jennifer said. "He eats like a horse and looks like a pencil."

"Someday it will catch up with him," Mr. Winston said with a chuckle, patting his own middle. "Believe me."

Lexi stood up. "I think I'll start cleaning up. Since Dmitri did all this work, I thought maybe the guys would like to do the dishes." She smiled broadly at Matt, Todd, and Egg.

They could hardly argue. With a sigh, Todd stood up and started picking up glasses and silverware. When Dmitri rose to help them, Lexi held out her hands.

"Oh no, you don't. It's your turn to have some fun. Let these guys do it."

"I think that's a great idea," Mrs. Winston said. "Dmitri, come with us girls into the living room and tell us more about your country."

Dmitri's eyes brightened. He looked at the girls and said, "Would you like to learn about the dancing in my country? I would like to show you *Syrtaki*. It is a very happy dance, usually danced by Greek men. There are also slow dances like the *Tsamikos*. They tell stories—usually sad ones."

"It isn't like dancing in this country at all, is it?" Binky asked.

"Probably not. The fast dances that are done by the men usually have complicated footwork and much leaping into the air. When the men dance, they wear pleated skirts and shirts with billowing sleeves. Often they wear a bolero and a tasseled hat."

"They wear costumes for dancing?"

Dmitri nodded.

"What do the women wear?" Lexi asked.

"Usually long, full skirts and big, billowy shirts as well. Greek dances are fun and very beautiful. Many dancers perform in competitions. We also have many festivals at which people dance. Come, I'll show you."

The girls followed him into the living room and sat in a circle as Dmitri pulled the coffee table into a corner to make room. Then he picked up a cassette tape that was lying on the stereo and slid it into the player. The room filled with music, and Dmitri, an intense expression on his face, began to dance. The girls were transfixed at the intricate footwork and high leaps Dmitri made as he danced. When he was finished, they clapped loudly.

"That was absolutely incredible!" Peggy breathed.

"No wonder there are dance competitions," Binky said. "You have to be an athlete to do that sort of thing."

"You are going to have to do that again," Mrs. Winston said firmly. "When I have the video camera out, I want to tape that so we can watch it when you're no longer here."

Dmitri blushed beneath his olive complexion. "You flatter me too much."

By then the guys were drifting in from the kitchen. "We heard all the fun out here. You girls just didn't want us around, did you?" Egg accused.

"Dmitri was just showing us how to dance," Lexi said.

By the end of the evening, they were all exhausted. One by one they drifted out, thanking Dmitri for the wonderful meal. Only Lexi and Jennifer stayed behind to do the final cleaning up.

"You can go," Lexi assured Jennifer. "This won't take long."

"Oh no. I'll help." Jennifer looked dismayed at the thought of leaving.

Lexi and Todd exchanged glances. Jennifer didn't like kitchen duty *that* much. There was obviously another reason for staying.

"I'll help you with the dishes," Todd offered.

"And I'll help Dmitri straighten these rooms." Jennifer indicated the dining and living rooms.

When Lexi and Todd got to the kitchen, they both burst out laughing.

"When did she get so domestic?" Todd asked.

"About the time Dmitri decided to cook."

"She's really fallen hard for him, hasn't she?"

"I hope not *too* hard." Lexi began wiping down the counters with a dish cloth. "Dmitri has to go back to his own country eventually, and where will that leave her?"

"Jennifer? She's tough."

"That's how much you know. She's a softie!"

"Are we talking about the same girl?" Todd teased. But when they were done, he took Lexi by the hand and said, "Come on, let's check up on those two."

The dining room had been restored to order and the lights lowered. It took a moment for Lexi to see Dmitri and Jennifer sitting together on the couch, talking quietly. Lexi could see by the glow in Jennifer's eyes that the conversation was agreeing with her. Her eyes dimmed at Lexi and Todd's approach.

"We were just talking about school," Jennifer said. She sounded a little defensive.

"Great. Can we join you?" Todd dropped onto the love seat and indicated that Lexi should join him.

From the corner of her eye, Lexi saw Dmitri's hand covering Jennifer's. Reluctantly, Jennifer pulled away. Lexi felt as though they were intruding.

"I guess I'd better go," Jennifer said without enthusiasm. "Mom will be expecting me."

"I'll walk you home," Dmitri offered. "It is not so far." To Todd he said, "I'll be back in a few minutes."

Jennifer's expression lit with pleasure.

After they had left, Todd turned to Lexi. "What do you think about that?"

"I think Dmitri is very polite but uneducated in the ways of women."

"Why do you say that?"

"Did you see how Jennifer was looking at him? She's falling—hard. And Minda is circling, too—getting closer and closer to Dmitri."

"And he's encouraging them both, you think?" Todd deduced.

"He's being nice to both. But sooner or later, if

Minda has her way, he'll have to choose between them." Lexi sighed. "Jennifer's my friend. I don't want to see her hurt."

Todd groaned a little. "Maybe it's a good thing Dmitri won't be here long."

"Maybe. But he'll be here long enough to see what happens when two girls like the same guy!"

"Poor Dmitri. I hope he doesn't regret ever leaving Greece!"

———————

Dmitri was as good as his word. He returned within half an hour.

"That was fast," Todd commented.

Dmitri grinned. "I gave her a ride on the back of your bike."

"Where do you get your energy?" Lexi asked as she sank deeper into the seat. "I'm tired, and I didn't even have to do all the work cooking like you did. Aren't you exhausted?"

"Although I love to cook, it is a great deal of work," he admitted.

"Thank you for being generous with everything you know," Lexi said. "I'm glad you came to stay with Todd and his family."

"I'm glad, too," Dmitri said. "Todd has been better than a brother to me." Then he smiled at Lexi. "It's been so good for me to be here in America. I've learned so much about your culture."

Lexi hesitated for a moment, as if she were considering her next words. "Speaking of cultures, there is something else I would like to know," she admitted. "But it seems kind of personal."

"There's nothing too personal for me," Dmitri said. "What would you like to know?"

"I'm curious about the religion in Greece. Is it like ours or . . ." She drifted into silence. Lexi's faith was so important to her that she wanted everyone to know about Jesus Christ.

"Religion is a very important part of life in Greece," Dmitri answered. "Every village has at least one church. Some have several, and they're usually whitewashed and have a bell tower. There are huge cathedrals and also tiny brick chapels. The majority of the people are Greek Orthodox. It is an ancient church believed to have originated with the apostles."

"How fascinating!" Lexi leaned forward in her chair.

"In Greece, our constitution gives us freedom of religion, just like here in America."

"Tell me about your church," Lexi encouraged.

"We have church on Sunday mornings, although the services are longer than yours."

"Really?"

"Yes, sometimes our services last for three hours."

"Three hours!" Todd yelped. "How can you stay awake that long?"

Dmitri laughed. "It is not hard. Normally we stand through our church services, the women on the left side and the men on the right. The children cluster around the floor at the front."

"I guess I'll never complain about the pews in

our church again," Todd blurted.

"The biblical Saint Paul brought the Christian religion to Greece in the first century," Dmitri explained. "Because Paul traveled through Greece and preached Christianity, he founded the first Christian church in all of Europe."

"Awesome," Lexi breathed. "To live in the country where Paul himself preached."

"Our country takes its religion very seriously. Easter is our most important feast day, and during Lent we give up meat and other things. It is a very exciting time for our family because my father's and mother's relatives come home. Neither of my parents go to work during Easter week. From Palm Sunday to Good Friday, there are services in our church every night. On Easter Eve, people everywhere in our country carry unlit candles to church services. When midnight comes, even the lights of the church are extinguished. It is a wonderful time when after midnight the Easter candle is carried in. One by one we light our candles, until the church is bright with the glow of the flames."

Lexi listened breathlessly, imagining the beauty of the scene.

"Then we go outside," Dmitri continued, "to the words *Khristos aesti*. Those words mean 'Christ has risen.'" Dmitri's eyes glowed as he explained the service. "The church bells begin to ring, firecrackers light the sky, and people cry and embrace each other and shout with joy."

"And this all happens after midnight on Easter?" Todd was amazed. "You mean we're home sleeping until our sunrise service at church, and you're celebrating all night?"

Dmitri nodded. "My mother always prepares a feast and serves it after our church service. About two or three in the morning we have a special soup that she serves only on Easter. She serves it with a loaf of bread, and for dessert we have cakes. It is the same every year."

"Then do you go to bed?" Todd asked.

"Only for a little while because when we get up, we must roast a lamb on the outside spit. Every family in the village does it, and when people walk by we always greet them with the words 'Christ is risen.' Sometimes we invite them to join us for lamb and the red-tinted eggs the children like so much."

"That's so great," Lexi said. "It sounds like a much more fitting celebration of Easter."

"Lots better than marshmallow bunnies and candied eggs so sweet you get cavities just from looking at them," Todd added.

"It is a joyous holiday in Greece," Dmitri agreed. "But why not? Easter brings us very happy news."

"I just *have* to visit there someday," Lexi said with determination. "And I want to be there on Easter."

"Then you must come to our house," Dmitri said. "My family would love to have you."

"Speaking of family," Lexi said with a sigh. "I suppose I should go home and see mine." She glanced at her watch. "It's getting late." She stood up. "Thank you, Dmitri, for a wonderful evening."

He nodded shyly as if he was embarrassed by all the praise he'd been getting.

Todd pulled the keys out of his pocket. "Do you want to ride along, Dmitri, while I take Lexi home?"

Dmitri shook his head. "No, I'm going to bed." He grinned impishly. "And from now on, I will appreciate my mother's cooking and all the work it takes much, much more!"

Chapter Six

Lexi picked up the phone on the third ring. It was Egg.

"Lexi, you've got to help me!" he pleaded.

"Is something wrong?" Egg and Binky seemed to invite crisis.

"Angela's birthday is coming up soon, and I want to have a surprise party for her."

"How nice!" Lexi exclaimed.

"Well, she *is* my girlfriend. I want to do something special for her. She's been kind of down lately. I thought a birthday party would cheer her up. Binky said she'd help me, too. Maybe you guys could plan it. I don't know much about giving parties."

"Where do you want to have it?" Lexi asked.

"At Angela's apartment."

"Are you sure it's okay?"

"Yes, I called her mother just before I called you. She said it's fine. That means we can have a surprise party. We'll all go to Angela's while she's out on an errand or something and surprise her when she comes home. Cool, huh?"

"I think it's a great idea, and it's really nice of

Angela's mom to let us do that. Maybe Peggy, Jennifer, and Anna Marie can help out, too. I'll ask them if they want to come to my house after school tomorrow to make the plans."

"Great!" There was relief in Egg's voice. "I don't want to blow this. Angela's really a special girl, and she needs a boost right now. Thanks, Lexi. You're a real pal."

———

"Don't look now, but trouble is coming this way," Binky hissed.

That, of course, meant that everyone at the table turned to see what Binky was talking about. Minda and Dmitri were walking through the cafeteria together. Her face was animated as she spoke, and she looked exceptionally pretty in her teal blue sweater and black pants.

Jennifer gripped the sides of her tray and pressed her lips into a tight line.

"Any comments?" Binky prodded.

Lexi nudged her nosy friend under the table, but it was too late. The question was already out.

"Why is it that Minda gets everything she wants?" Jennifer blurted.

"He's not like a new dress or a pair of shoes," Todd pointed out. "And she didn't exactly pluck him off a tree."

"No, but she's got her eye on him, and once that happens, you know as well as I do what that means." Jennifer shoved the food around on her plate. "There'll be no chance for me."

"I don't know about that," Todd said. "I think

you already have something Minda doesn't have—
and you'll have it even if Minda 'gets' him."

"What's that?"

"His friendship," Todd said matter-of-factly.
"And isn't that better, anyway?"

Jennifer pursed her lips and furrowed her brow
as she thought about what Todd had said. Then she
smiled a little. "True. Dmitri and I get along great.
That should drive Minda *nuts!*"

————

The girls gathered at Lexi's house after school.
They sat around the dining-room table, each with a
piece of paper and a pencil, all eager to make plans
for Angela's surprise party.

"Okay," Lexi said. "Since we have the time and
place set, we'd better decide what kind of food we're
having."

"Munchies," Jennifer said firmly. "We definitely
have to have munchies. You know, chips and dip,
pretzels, nuts, mini pizzas, and chocolate. Angela
loves chocolate."

"I've got an idea," Lexi said. "Maybe Dmitri
would make that tzatziki again. We could have that
with pita bread."

"Just talking about this is making me hungry,"
Peggy said. "Why don't Jennifer and Dmitri take
care of the food? Anna Marie and I can call everyone
and tell them about the party. Lexi, what do you
want to be in charge of?"

"I've been thinking about that," Lexi told them,
tapping her fingers on her knee. "Why don't we pool

our money together for a gift and get her something special?"

"Good idea," Anna Marie said. "What do you have in mind?"

Lexi looked a little embarrassed. "It sounds kind of silly, but every time we go shopping at the mall, Angela stops at the makeup counter in the department stores. She always says that someday, when she has the money, she is going to have a makeover. Maybe we could give her a gift certificate at the department store and make an appointment for her."

"What a great idea, Lexi. I'd love a gift like that." Peggy's eyes sparked with interest. "I can hardly wait to see her expression when she finds out."

————

Saturday night, Lexi and Binky were the first to arrive at the Hardys' apartment. Lexi was carrying the birthday cake her mother had baked for the occasion. Binky carried a bag full of streamers and balloons.

"What a beautiful cake," Mrs. Hardy gasped when Lexi took the top off the plastic container.

"My mom really got into it," Lexi said. "It's a three-layer chocolate cake with cream cheese frosting."

"But look at the decorations," Mrs. Hardy said.

Mrs. Leighton had drawn a little scene with colored frosting that looked like a girl's bedroom. She had painted a tiny vanity with a miniature mirror. Lying on the vanity were a real pair of silver earrings. Mrs. Leighton had also painted in a stereo, a pair of sneakers, and a tiny CD.

"I wish I were artistic like that," Binky said admiringly. "I'm not even sure what we should do with this." She held out the bag. "There are some streamers, some candles . . ."

"Here, I'll help you," Mrs. Hardy said. "We want to be done by the time Angela returns."

"Where is she?"

"I sent her to the store for groceries. I promised to make her favorite meal for her birthday." Mrs. Hardy grinned. "She doesn't know everything's already cooked."

"But that means we don't have much time. I hope the others come soon. . . ." Lexi's voice trailed away as the doorbell rang.

One by one Angela's friends entered, each carrying whatever item of food Binky had suggested they bring. Dmitri and Todd arrived with the tzatziki and a plate full of pita bread. Matt came with a case of soda.

Peggy and Mrs. Hardy hung streamers while the guys grew red-faced blowing up balloons. Binky had made banners on her computer, which they hung around the room. Egg flitted from group to group, trying to help but only making things worse.

"Settle down, Eggo," Todd finally ordered. "You're a nervous wreck, and all you're doing is slowing us down."

"I'm sorry. I just can't help it," Egg said with a sigh. "For some reason I'm really nervous about this. I hope she likes it."

"Quiet! I hear someone coming up the stairs."

Everyone dived for the preplanned places they were to hide. Binky, Peggy, Jennifer, and Matt crouched behind the couch. Anna Marie and Tim headed for the closet. Mrs. Hardy disappeared behind the door of her bedroom. All was silent when Angela's key turned in the lock. She stopped in the doorway, taking in the decorations, as the room erupted with yells and cheers.

Egg was slightly off key as he led everyone in singing "Happy Birthday."

Angela stood in the doorway, both hands clutching grocery bags, her mouth wide open in amazement. "You guys," she said. "How did you . . . why . . . how? I can't believe it!"

"Are you surprised?" Binky asked.

"Very. This is so great!" Angela appeared to be genuinely happy. It was a nice change from the past few weeks.

Lexi stole a look at Egg. It was obvious that he was happy, too.

———

They had finished the food and games when Angela asked Dmitri, "What are birthdays like in Greece?"

"Not like this," he said. "We do not celebrate birthdays like you do in this country. Although we recognize them, they are not as important as *name days*. It is the day celebrating the saint after whom you are named. We take presents and sweet cakes to our friends. Sometimes whole villages have name days and celebrate together with food and music. It is more like a festival than a birthday party. I also think we celebrate Christmas differently than you do here in America."

"How's that?" Todd asked.

"Our families get together at Christmas, but it is a very religious holiday, and we do not exchange a lot of gifts. Rather, it is a children's festival. In the villages, there are bonfires after dark to remind us that the shepherds near Bethlehem saw the star that first Christmas."

"That's a great idea," Peggy said. "We should do that."

"And then on Christmas morning we go to church. Sometimes gifts are exchanged, but usually families wait until St. Basil's Day. It is the day you call New Year's Day."

"Speaking of gifts," Lexi said, "I think it's time Angela opened hers."

"You're giving me gifts, too? Oh, you don't have to. This party is enough."

"Just a couple." Lexi handed her an exquisitely wrapped box that was long and flat. Angela looked at it quizzically, wondering what could be inside.

"It's from all of us," Lexi said, gesturing at the others in the room. "We hope you like it."

Angela undid the bow and carefully unwrapped the box and lifted the lid. She unfolded a single sheet of tissue paper to see the gift certificate inside. She read the words, and as she did her eyes grew wide.

"I've always wanted this. How did you know?"

Lexi laughed. "I've been to the mall with you enough times to figure it out. We decided that rather than get you little things, we'd all put our pennies together and buy you something special."

"Oh, I love it. I just love it." Angela jumped up and went around the room hugging every single person. At last she came to Egg.

"Don't hug me for that," he said. "I'm not in on the gift. I brought my own." He handed her an envelope.

"Well, I know from the last gift that good things come in small packages," Angela said as she freed the glued flap and peeked inside.

"Egg, you didn't!" she squealed as she pulled out two tickets. "The ballet?"

Egg blushed as all the guys stared at him. "Hey, don't look at me like that! I heard her tell Mrs. Waverly once that one thing she wanted to do was go to the ballet. There's a troupe coming to the college next month, and I just thought—"

"Egg McNaughton, that is the sweetest thing you've ever done." Angela threw herself on him and gave him a bear hug while the girls clapped.

"He must really like you," Matt growled. "The ballet . . . yuck."

Everyone was laughing and congratulating Egg on his creativity. Angela had tears in her eyes as she thanked her friends for what they'd done.

"Things are getting a little too emotional," Todd said. He clapped his hands. "I think we need another round of entertainment." They all turned to him curiously. "Dmitri showed the girls Greek dancing the other night at my place, but we guys missed it. What do you say, Dmitri? Want to give us a lesson?"

"I don't have any music," Dmitri said hesitantly.

Todd produced a tape from his pocket. "But I do."

While the girls watched, Dmitri gave the guys their first lesson. Mrs. Hardy, after watching a few moments of the comical sight, disappeared into her room. When she returned, Lexi noticed that she had changed out of the jeans and sweat shirt she had been wearing. She now had on a slim denim skirt and an attractive pink blouse. Her hair was combed back from her face, and she looked very pretty.

"You look nice," Lexi commented.

"Thank you. If you kids don't mind, I'll just slip out for a while," she said softly. Then she blushed. "I have a date."

Angela turned around and saw her mother talking to Lexi. As Lexi watched, Angela's happy mood seemed to evaporate into thin air. Her lips turned downward and she frowned.

"You're leaving?" Her tone was harsh.

"Just for an hour or two. I promise it won't be long."

At that moment the doorbell rang, and Angela watched as her mother went to answer it.

A tall, very handsome man stood on the other side of the door. "Hi, are you ready?" he began. Then he saw all the activity inside the apartment. "A party?" He looked at Angela's mother. "Are you sure you want to leave?"

Mrs. Hardy hesitated for a moment, then shook her head. "It's all right. The kids need some private time." She looked pointedly at her daughter.

"Happy birthday, Angela," the man said. "I

brought you a little gift." He placed a small bear clutching a bottle of perfume in its furry arms on the table next to the door.

Angela barely acknowledged the gesture.

"Come on. Let's go," Mrs. Hardy said. "I'll be home in a couple hours," she said to Angela, then closed the door behind her.

The party suddenly seemed over. Angela's mood changed from lighthearted to silent and angry. Confused, the kids drifted out one by one until only Todd, Lexi, Egg, Binky, and Dmitri were left behind.

"Listen, Angela," Egg began, "I'm sorry you're upset about your mom and that guy."

"I don't want to talk about it," Angela said sharply.

"Okay, we don't have to." Egg tried to appease her.

"In fact, I think I want to go to bed now," Angela said, tears filling her eyes.

"At this time of night? It's still early. We could rent a movie and—"

"I'm tired, Egg, really," Angela cut Egg off. "Thanks for everything, but I think you'd all better go."

They left stunned and confused, not quite sure how their wonderful party had turned to such a disaster.

Chapter Seven

"Are you as bored as I am?" Binky asked as Lexi answered the phone.

"I don't know. How bored are you?"

"Horribly bored. I even did my homework. I was that desperate."

"My, this must be serious," Lexi said, laughing.

"Well, it's true. I didn't have all that much homework, and there's nothing good on television. Mom told me I couldn't rent any more movies this month, and the only thing left to do is clean my room."

"Well, we can't let that happen," Lexi said. "Where's Egg? He usually entertains you."

"He's playing a game of basketball at the school. It's open gym tonight."

"Oh, I'd forgotten about that," Lexi said. "I suppose Todd and Dmitri are there, too."

"Do you want to go watch them?"

"You mean you think that wouldn't be boring?"

There was a pause as Binky considered Lexi's question. "True, but it would be less boring than sitting at home. Can you pick me up?"

"I'll be there in fifteen minutes."

———

They walked into the gymnasium to see a group of sweating, red-faced guys pounding up and down the basketball court. Egg was the sweatiest and most red-faced of all.

"I think your brother needs to get in shape," Lexi whispered to Binky.

"Tell me about it. He thinks he *is* in shape. But we don't dare say too much about it because Egg went on that crazy weight lifting binge once before."

Lexi remembered all too well. Not only had Egg gone into weight lifting, he had considered taking steroids to bulk up his muscles. It had been a scary time for all of them.

Tonight Egg was on the red team. They wore red sleeveless pullovers over their shirts to designate their team. Todd's was the blue team. Dmitri was playing with Todd, while Tim Anders and Jerry Randall were Egg's teammates.

"Why don't they have an open gym night for girls?" Binky growled. "It's just not fair."

"Bink, they do. You just never come."

"They do? Oh." Binky blushed. "Maybe I shouldn't talk about how physically unfit my brother is when I'm just as bad or worse." Then she looked around. "You'd think they'd sell popcorn or something on nights like this."

Lexi threw her hands into the air. Binky was impossible, and there was not a thing she could do about it.

"I'm surprised," Binky observed. "They're playing pretty fast, aren't they? I always thought this was just a lazy night for them, shooting a few hoops, doing some visiting."

"Guys don't visit, Binky. They play games. You know that."

"Look, Egg just stole the ball. He's taking it to the far end of the court to make a lay-up." And that was just what Egg was doing—loping away from the rest of the players, his eyes on the far basket and a large grin on his face for making the steal.

"Whoa, he's going to try to stuff it," Binky squealed as Egg launched himself into the air toward the basket. The ball fell through the hoop and hit the floor. Egg did the same, but *he* didn't bounce. Instead he crumpled, his ankle twisted at an unnatural angle. The girls heard his sharp cry of pain from the bleachers.

"He's hurt!" Binky jumped to her feet.

Lexi put her hand on the girl's arm. "Leave him alone. Todd's checking him out. You don't want to embarrass him in case it isn't serious. He'd hate that."

"But isn't he making an awful lot of noise for someone who might not be hurt?"

Egg was moaning and groaning.

"Is he being dramatic or is that for real?" Minda Hannaford appeared beside the two girls. She'd come to watch Dmitri play ball.

"Who can tell with Egg?" Binky said.

Then Todd looked up and waved to Lexi and Binky. Minda followed them.

"I think we better take him over to the open clinic at the mall and have a doctor look at this."

"I'll have to be on crutches," Egg moaned. "Or a wheelchair. Ohhh nooo."

"Egg, calm down," Todd ordered. "You twisted your ankle. You might have sprained it."

"I might have broken it," Egg retorted.

"That, too, but standing around here discussing it isn't going to help. Come on. Let us help you up and get you to the car. Lexi, you better find Coach Drummond and tell him what happened."

Lexi ran to do just that and then joined the little entourage as they hobbled toward Todd's car. "Coach Drummond wants to know if he should come along," she panted, almost out of breath.

Todd looked to Egg, who shook his head. "We can handle it."

"Okay, then he says to be sure to tell the clinic it was an accident that happened at school. I'll go back and tell him what we're doing." Lexi had time to run all the way into the school and come out again while they were still loading Egg into the car. He was hollering at the top of his lungs. He settled down to mild fussing as Lexi, Binky, and Dmitri climbed into the backseat from the driver's side of Todd's car. He was just muttering to himself by the time they reached the clinic. The nurse reacted immediately by putting him in an examining room while Binky called their parents for permission for the doctor to treat him.

"Can we stay with him?" Binky asked.

The nurse looked at the foursome, Todd and Dmitri still in their shorts and shirts and team pullovers from the basketball court. "Those examining rooms are pretty crowded," she said with a smile. "I think it might be better if you stay out here in the waiting room. Besides, I'm sure the doctor will order some X-rays. Egg will be leaving the examining room for that. Why don't you just sit down or walk around the mall for a while and come back to see how's he doing."

"We'll wait." Binky plunked herself into one of the chairs. She picked up a magazine and thumbed through it. "It actually *is* true. There are no new magazines in doctors' offices. Look at this—1996, and all the recipes are torn out. This is no fun." She threw the magazine down. Then her little face crumpled and tears leaked onto her cheeks.

"Binky, what's wrong?"

"What if his ankle is broken and we didn't believe him? I would feel so terrible."

"Binky, what a silly thing to worry about. We took him to the clinic, didn't we?"

"But what we said about Egg being so dramatic all the time . . ."

"Well, he *is* dramatic, Binky," Todd said calmly. "I've seen him get a sliver in his hand and act like someone had stabbed him through the heart with a sword."

Dmitri surprised them all by starting to laugh. He held his sides and laughed so hard he doubled over. Finally, when his laughter had died down, he wiped his eyes and said, "I'm sorry. Egg's injury is not funny but . . ." He looked up pleadingly at Binky as if to ask for her forgiveness and understanding. "Your brother is a very funny guy."

Todd, Lexi, and Binky stared at Dmitri for a moment, and then they, too, burst into laughter.

Binky waved a hand in the air. "Don't worry about saying that, Dmitri. He is a funny guy."

"But a nice one," Lexi added. "Really, there's no one with a kinder heart than Egg."

"I have realized that," Dmitri said. "I'm glad that he is my friend, but he has the most interesting reactions to things."

"That's a nice way of putting it," Todd said. The laughter had released the tension in the room.

Dmitri, pacing the small confines of the room, stopped in front of a huge poster on the wall. "Look," he said, pointing at the words. "This is the Hippocratic Oath."

"Is that anything like Hippocrates?" Binky asked. "He's an ancient Greek guy, right?"

"Very good," Dmitri said. "He was a famous doctor in ancient Greece. He outlined rules of conduct between doctors and patients, which are still followed today."

"Wow," Binky marveled. "Imagine that, after all these years."

"You come from an impressive place, Dmitri," Todd finally said. "Those early Greeks must have been some smart men."

Before he could say more, there was a commotion at the door, and Egg came hobbling through with the aid of crutches. He kept his foot held off the ground, and it was tightly taped in bandages.

"Is it broken?" Binky asked.

"No, just a nasty sprain," the nurse said. "Egg has a list of instructions in his pocket that include taking some aspirin tonight for pain."

Egg looked at her fearfully. "Will there be a lot of pain?"

The nurse smiled at him. "Let's hope not."

Egg looked very pale and anxious.

"Come on, we'll help you to the car." Todd and Dmitri moved to his side and cautiously ushered Egg through the door.

———

By the time they had him settled in the living room of his house, they all knew that Binky was in trouble. Egg had already asked for three different pillows, ice water, a soda, and a glass of pineapple juice. Binky was running back and forth from the kitchen and the upstairs like a little mouse scurrying around.

"And the remote for the TV, please," Egg said in a helpless and pleading voice. Binky ran to get it.

"Maybe I'd feel better if I read a book," Egg suggested, and off Binky went to find the latest mystery thriller Egg had been reading. By the time she got to the chair with that, he said, "Did that sports magazine come today? I can't remember having seen it. I think I'd like to look at that."

Todd exchanged a glance with Lexi and said, "I think we'd better go." When they were outside, he started to shake his head. Then he, Lexi, and Dmitri started to laugh.

"Poor Binky," they said in unison.

"Egg is going to play his injury for all it's worth," Todd said as they left the driveway.

"As much as Binky enjoys being a mother hen, I'll bet he keeps her running for at least a week."

———————

But Todd's prediction did not come true. When he and Lexi arrived at Egg's the next afternoon to see how he was doing, Binky opened the door.

"Hi, come on in," she said. In the background they could hear Egg yelling.

"I'm dying of thirst in here. Water, I need water."

"What's going on?" Todd indicated the living room.

"Oh, he wants me to wait on him," Binky said without sympathy. "But I'm not going to because he's not doing anything for me."

"Well, well, it looks like patient and nurse have already had a little spat."

"Water, I need water."

Binky ignored him. "He won't help me with my computer," she said. "I told him the least he could do today while he was just sitting around was load some of my software. And did he do it? No. He said he was in too much pain to get from the chair to the computer. Ha! He was all over the house today, even though Mom and Dad both told him he had to stay put. He was in the bathroom and the kitchen and even upstairs."

"How do you know?" Lexi asked, surprised.

"Because he left the sink all grungy in the bathroom, and because he's got a pillow behind his back that was on his bed this morning. And I had three candy bars hidden in the freezer that were for a special occasion, and two of them are gone."

"You really are the Sherlock Holmes of Cedar River," Todd observed. "Nothing gets by you."

"I wish. This computer has gotten by me totally. I do know one thing, though." Binky brightened. "I learned how to send e-mail." She gave an unexpected dreamy sigh. "It's great!"

"E-mail is great?" Todd looked at her. "What have you been using it for? To send love letters?"

To their surprise, Binky blushed.

"You've got to be kidding," Todd blurted when he realized that somehow he had hit the mark.

Hearing Todd's outburst, Egg managed to make his way to the doorway to listen in on their conversation.

"Not love letters, really. Just letters, sort of."

"To who?" Lexi stared at her friend.

"Oh, just to this guy I met on-line," Binky said casually, more casually than she obviously felt.

"When did this happen?" Egg glared at his sister. "You met a guy on-line and didn't tell me?"

"You wouldn't help me with my computer, so why should I tell you anything about it?" Binky glared at her brother.

Egg waved a dismissing hand. "I don't think she could manage it," he said.

"I can, too. I'm very good at it. We met in a chat room, and we've e-mailed each other a couple of times."

"A chat room? Aren't those places where weird people go?"

"Not necessarily," Binky said. "This one is for high school students. Tom is a very nice guy."

"So, it's 'Tom,' is it? How do you know that 'Tom' isn't a forty-year-old man who can't make any friends his own age?" Egg said bluntly.

Binky glared at him.

"And what does Harry think of this?" Lexi asked. Harry was Binky's sometimes boyfriend who was away at school.

"Harry doesn't mind. I wrote to him on e-mail, too. We both think it's the greatest invention ever."

"I can't believe I'm hearing this," Lexi said.

"I'm not as dumb as you people think I am," Binky said primly. "You expect me to be dizzy all the time, but I'm not."

"We don't expect you to be dizzy," Lexi corrected her.

"I do," Egg said cheerfully. "I think she's making it up."

Binky looked horrified.

"She hasn't met a guy, and she's not writing to Harry. She doesn't know how to work that computer."

"Edward McNaughton, I'll show you. Come on," Binky challenged.

Egg looked startled. "What do you want me to do?"

"Get up off that couch and I'll show you how to talk to them."

"I don't know Tom."

"No, but you do know Harry. Come on."

Binky went to the other side of the family room where the computer sat and switched it on. Egg, too curious to ignore this turn of events, struggled to his feet with Todd's help, took his crutches, and swung himself toward the computer. Binky was already typing a message to the e-mail address on the screen.

"Harry's usually on his computer this time of day. Maybe we'll get lucky and he'll check his messages right away." Binky typed as she spoke, "Hi, Harry. This is Binky. Todd, Lexi, and Egg are here with me. Do you have anything you want to say to them?" Binky sent the message and then went into a chat room to show the others.

They had been exploring the Internet for a while when an e-mail came back that said, "Hi, Binky. Hello, Todd, Lexi, Egg. What's up? I've got lots of studying to do. Two papers and a test due this week. Is anything happening in Cedar River?"

"She *can* do it!" Egg's eyes were wide and his voice awestruck. "She can actually do it."

"So there, Mr. Smarty Pants," she said triumphantly. "What do you think of that?"

"I guess I have to apologize," Egg said. "You surprised me, you really did."

"It looks like you're getting another message," Todd said.

"Hmmm, I wonder who that could be." Binky pulled the message onto the screen. It was from the mysterious Tom.

"That's the guy you said you met on-line. What does he want?" Egg asked.

Binky turned away from the screen to glare at her brother. "Maybe it's a private message."

"Private? I'm telling Mom and Dad if you're getting any private messages on the computer."

"Oh, all right." Binky pulled up the note. " 'Dear Binky,' " she read aloud. " 'Wouldn't it be great if we could meet sometime? I know that I'm all the way out in California, but maybe we could meet somewhere? Do you ever go on vacation? Think about it. Tom.' "

"Wow," Binky said. "That's the first time he's ever said anything like that."

"He sounds interested in you," Todd said.

"What kind of a creep is it anyway who asks you to meet him when you're on vacation? You're a high school kid! Do you know how many states apart you guys are?" Egg demanded.

"He's never said anything like that before. We've just talked about music and stuff." Binky stared at the screen, puzzled.

Lexi shivered. "I think it's creepy. What if he's a weirdo, Binky? Now he sounds interested in you. You didn't give him your address, did you?"

"No, of course not. I'm not that stupid." Then Binky reconsidered. "But what's so bad about this? Maybe he just thinks I'm nice and wants to meet me. What if he's *not* a weirdo?"

"How can you tell until it's too late?" Todd said seriously. "Binky, I think you'd better quit talking to him. I don't like this. It feels funny to me."

"And maybe you guys worry too much."

"Maybe we do, Binky, but every once in a while you hear stories about guys stalking people they've met on the computer."

"That's not the usual thing."

"No, but it does happen. My mom uses e-mail a lot through her work and she surfs the Net all the time, but she always hooks up with people who are in her field or with people doing research in an area she's interested in. She says you should make your friends face-to-face, not on the Internet."

"I don't know if I agree with her one hundred percent," Binky said as she frowned at the message. "But I guess you're right. This feels kind of creepy to me, too." She deleted the letter as Todd and Egg moved toward the kitchen. "Maybe I'll just stick to being friends with you guys for a while."

"I think that's a great idea," Lexi said.

"Still," Binky mused. "It's kind of romantic to meet someone like this. . . ."

"Binky, use your brain."

Binky was going to retort when the girls heard a big thump coming from the kitchen, where the boys had gone. When they got there, Todd was helping Egg off the floor.

"What happened?" Lexi gasped.

"Egg fell down."

"We can see that."

"He got his crutches tangled in the leg of the kitchen chair."

"Oh, Egg. You're going to have to practice with those things." Binky turned to Todd. "He can't use these crutches right, but he refuses to give up."

"But then I'd have to sit down all the time," Egg protested.

"I thought that's what you liked," Binky pointed out. "Here, let us help you." Binky began to dust off her brother. "If you aren't careful, you're going to sprain something else. But now that we're all here, do you want me to make you shakes?"

Egg brightened considerably at the prospect. "It may not do anything for my ankle," he said. "But it would certainly improve my attitude."

Chapter Eight

Creaking chairs, shuffling feet, coughing, and sneezing were the only sounds in the music room as Mrs. Waverly stared at her chorus, hands on hips, hair slightly askew. Usually a patient woman, even Mrs. Waverly was frustrated today.

"Why is everyone so restless?" she wondered aloud. "I feel like I'm directing a can of worms with all that squirming and wriggling going on."

Someone in the soprano section giggled at the image.

"Worse yet, today no one seems to be on pitch." Mrs. Waverly scanned the room. Lexi tried to sit still and look attentive, but it was difficult to pay attention today. It had been a hard week for everyone, with lots of tests and more homework than anyone should have to do. Then Mrs. Waverly's puzzled expression turned to a smile.

"We could keep on pounding away at this piece," she said. "But my instincts tell me what you really need today is a break." There was a collective sigh in the room.

"And I have an idea for something that might be a fun change of pace." She turned to Dmitri. "Since everyone seems to fight learning this song in German, perhaps you'd like to teach us some Greek phrases. Maybe that will get everyone's mind going."

Dmitri grinned, catching on to Mrs. Waverly's idea. "You mean after hearing Greek, German will seem easy." The kids started to laugh.

"Come on, Dmitri. Talk to us in your language," someone in the back row called out.

Dmitri thought about it for only a moment, then he stood up. "I would be happy to."

"Good," Mrs. Waverly said appreciatively. "Maybe that will jump start the class, so to speak."

The kids were perking up already, seeing that Mrs. Waverly was not going to hold them to the tedious task she had set for them.

"Since there is no way you can begin to learn the Greek alphabet in one class," Dmitri began, "I will teach you to pronounce some phrases that you would use in Greece. For example, 'What's new?' is *ti nea?* 'So long' or 'good-bye' is *andio!*"

"That sounds like *adios* in Spanish!" Tim pointed out.

Dmitri had everyone laughing as he told them stories of practicing his English by watching television shows since he'd arrived in America. By the time they got around to working on the song Mrs. Waverly had assigned, everyone was in a much better mood.

———————

"It's been a long time since I've seen your grandmother," Todd commented as he and Lexi pulled up in his driveway late Saturday afternoon. "Do you think she recognized me?"

"It's hard to tell with Alzheimer's patients," Lexi admitted. "But I really think she did, Todd. Anyway, whoever she thought you were, she was glad to see you. Thanks for coming with me. Sometimes it's hard for me to go there and see how Grandmother's changed. Other times, she seems so much like herself. . . ." Lexi's voice trailed away. Her grandmother's illness had been hard on her family.

"I wonder what Dmitri has been doing all afternoon," Todd commented. "He said he had a lot of homework to get done."

"That doesn't sound like a very fun Saturday."

"No, it doesn't." Todd squinted as he looked toward the front room of his house. "Who's walking back and forth inside my living room?"

Lexi looked, too. "I don't know. Let's go find out."

When they walked in the front door, they discovered it was Dmitri pacing the floor, back and forth, back and forth, like some sort of frantic animal in a cage.

"What's wrong with you?" Todd asked.

Dmitri looked up. His expression was tense. "What time is it?" he asked.

"Almost six," Todd responded.

Dmitri began pacing again. "I can't decide if the clock is moving very slowly or very quickly," he muttered.

"Whoa." Todd walked across the room and put his hand on Dmitri's arm. "Settle down and tell us what's going on."

"I am nervous."

"Why? You seemed perfectly fine when Lexi and I left here a few hours ago."

Dmitri looked slightly sheepish. "Something has occurred since you left that has put me in some . . ." He searched for the word and finally came up with one. "Distress."

"What's that?" Todd immediately grew concerned. "Is it anything my parents can help you with?"

"Oh no, nothing like that. It is just that I got a phone call."

Lexi stepped forward. "Not from Greece? Everything's all right with your family, isn't it?"

"Fine, I am sure. The phone call was not from Greece. It was from Minda Hannaford."

"What's she doing calling and getting you all upset?"

Dmitri gave a lopsided smile. "I do not think she meant to make me upset. I think she meant to please me. She asked me to go out with her tonight."

Lexi and Todd stared at him in disbelief.

"Minda asked you on a date?"

Dmitri nodded. "Is it all right that I said yes? I did not want to seem rude and say no. And my parents did say that when I went to America I should learn American teenagers' ways. . . ." His voice trailed away just as Todd burst out laughing. Dmitri and Lexi both looked at him, shocked.

Todd laughed until he had to wipe a tear out of his eye and sit down on the edge of the couch. He was shaking his head and chuckling until Lexi poked at him with the toe of her shoe.

"What on earth is so funny?"

"Minda asked Dmitri out. *That's* what's so funny. You know how Minda is. She would never lower herself to asking one of us guys out. She usually has plenty of masculine attention. But I suppose she figured that since Dmitri is only here six weeks she might not have time to work her charms on him, so she decided to go straight to the point and ask him out. I think it's great. Funny."

Lexi was not nearly as amused as Todd. "It will probably upset Jennifer."

"I forgot about that," Todd murmured. "Ouch."

Dmitri didn't seem to understand the full significance of Lexi's statement. He looked with a puzzled expression from Lexi to Todd and back again.

"Never mind," Lexi said quickly. She glanced at Todd. "You know how Minda is."

Dmitri looked at her sharply. "How *is* Minda?"

Lexi sorted out her thoughts before saying, "Let's just say that Minda is a very strong-willed person. It doesn't surprise me. All of the Hi-Fives have been flirting with you. But I suppose Minda, as their ring leader, had first option to ask you out."

"You will have to explain—"

But Todd interrupted them to ask, "What are you doing?"

"We are going to a movie and then to a party."

"Where's the party?" Lexi asked.

"At Tressa's house," Dmitri said hesitantly.

"In other words, 'the works,' " Todd said. He was still chuckling.

Dmitri was not comforted by his attitude. "I do

not know what my parents would say about this. They are very strict. . . ." His voice trailed off. "Tell me more about Minda. I do not know her very well."

Lexi and Todd exchanged a glance, and in that moment they made an unspoken agreement.

"She's a very pretty girl," Lexi said. "But, of course, you can see that for yourself." She was wracking her brain for the good things she knew about Minda. Dmitri would have to find out the negative for himself. "And she's very bright. She's the fashion columnist for our school newspaper, the *Cedar River Review*. I guess you could call Minda a trendsetter in many ways."

"Yes, yes, but tell me about her family. In Greece, family is very important."

"Her father is wealthy," Todd said. "Minda is never short of money, but I don't think her home life is very good."

Lexi took up the story there. "As far as I know, Minda's parents are separated, and her dad has problems handling alcohol. I don't know much more about her family life. Minda doesn't usually talk about it. She doesn't like to show anyone the chinks in her armor. She wants everyone to think she's cool and strong. But I don't think it can be easy all the time, especially when her dad's been drinking."

Sympathy welled into Dmitri's beautiful brown eyes. "Then I am beginning to feel sorry for Minda," he said. "She has a hard time in her life."

"Oh, I wouldn't go so far as to start feeling sorry for her," Todd warned. "Minda knows how to handle herself. In fact," Todd said, breaking the unspoken agreement that he and Lexi had made at the beginning of this conversation, "she can be pretty mean if she wants to. Lexi knows that from experience."

Dmitri looked puzzled. "How?"

"Oh, Todd, don't go into that now."

"No, I think Dmitri should know. When Lexi first moved to Cedar River, Minda and her friends invited her to be part of the Hi-Fives, but when Lexi wouldn't take part in their secret little initiation, Minda decided to steer clear." Todd didn't mention that the girls wanted Lexi to shoplift something from a store or that Minda reacted negatively to Lexi's little brother, Ben.

"But Minda and I are getting along much better now," Lexi quickly added. "I think she's really mellowed toward me. Don't you, Todd?"

"Minda could be a really nice girl. That's why she's so frustrating sometimes. You'd just like to shake her and tell her to get rid of the attitude and just be herself."

Dmitri was listening to all of this intently. "So she can be nice and she can be cruel. She is both smart and beautiful, but she has a bad family life." He considered this for a moment. "It seems to me I have accepted a date with a very complicated girl."

Before their conversation could go any further, the doorbell rang. Dmitri nearly jumped out of his shoes. Todd began to chuckle again, but Lexi gave him a glare and made him turn away.

"Quit it. You're making Dmitri more nervous than he needs to be."

"But he needs to be plenty nervous," Todd whispered.

Dmitri, ignoring them both, went to the door

and opened it. Minda was framed in the doorway, wearing a skinny ribbed shirt of powder blue that exactly matched her eyes. She also wore a short denim skirt, which enhanced her long, shapely legs. On her feet she wore chunky shoes with high heels. Her hair was a cloud of curls around her face, and her makeup was flawlessly applied. Minda looked as though she had stepped off the pages of a magazine.

Dmitri seemed transfixed by the girl in front of him.

It was Lexi who stepped forward and said, "Wow, you look nice."

Minda did not seem surprised to see her there. "Thank you."

That woke Todd up as well. "You really do look great, Minda. Exceptional."

She batted her eyelashes at him. "I'm glad you like it."

"Yes, you are lovely," Dmitri echoed. "Come inside."

"I'd love to, but I don't think we have time," Minda said sweetly. She was on her best behavior this evening. "Especially not if we want to get to the early movie. It starts at seven. Have you had dinner?"

"No." Dmitri shook his head.

"Maybe we could go have a burger or something." She dangled her car keys in front of Dmitri. "I've got the Mercedes tonight." Then she turned to Todd and Lexi. "Do you want to join us?" They were shocked at Minda's politeness.

Todd recovered first. "Oh, no thanks. You and

Dmitri go and have a good time." Then Todd looked at Dmitri. "Remember my mom and dad's curfew," he said and then winked.

Looking slightly stunned, Dmitri followed Minda out of the house and to the car. After Todd had closed the door, he turned around and leaned against it, grinning broadly.

Seeing his face, Lexi broke into a peal of laughter.

"Who was that sweet, polite, attractive person we just met?" Todd said. "Could that be the Minda Hannaford we all know and love to hate?"

"Oh, don't be so hard on her, Todd. She was trying really hard. I think it's kind of sweet."

"Do you think the change is permanent?" Todd asked.

"I'm willing to believe that Minda has changed a little bit since I moved to Cedar River," she said with a smile. "And that's what I think she's changed—a little. Tonight I think we saw the person that Minda could be if she tried very hard, not the person she is."

"Evidently, Dmitri brings out the best in her," Todd said. "And I'm glad somebody does. Come on, let's go find my mom and see if she's got anything interesting on the stove for supper."

———

"I think I'm in love!"

Lexi stared at the telephone receiver she just picked up. "Who is this?" she demanded.

"It's me, Binky. Don't you recognize my voice?"

"Oh, I thought I did, but I don't recognize the words you said."

"I'm in love," Binky said emphatically. "I've met someone, and he's the neatest guy in the whole world."

"Didn't I just see you yesterday?" Lexi asked. "And I don't remember hearing a thing about your being in love or having met somebody. Besides, I thought you were supposed to stay home today and do housework. When did you even have time to meet someone?"

"On the Internet, of course. We've been talking for a couple of days, but today we had a two-hour conversation. It was so cool, Lexi, I just can't tell you."

"You talked two hours on the Internet?"

"It was neat. We told everything about ourselves, what we thought and about our interests. It was so great, I just loved it."

"And this phantom boyfriend of yours, he feels the same way about you?" Lexi frowned into the phone. Binky was going through Internet guys like Lexi went through tissues when she had a cold!

Binky hesitated. "Well, no, not exactly. I mean, we didn't really say that we liked each other, but I just know that this guy is perfect for me. He's kind and he's gentle and he's smart."

"Binky, didn't we already have this conversation once?"

"About the weirdos that could be in chat rooms?"

"Remember that last guy?"

"I know, Lexi, but this is different."

"How could this be different?" Lexi asked.

"Well, for one thing, he's from Brentwood."

"You mean the Brentwood where my cousin Sarah lives?"

"That's the one. He even says he knows Sarah! So you see, Lexi, this is no weirdo."

"I wouldn't count on it until I talk to my cousin." *But why worry? By that time Binky will have met somebody else!*

"Don't call her!" Binky was worried. "I guess I like being anonymous."

"What's wrong, Binky? You sound upset all of a sudden."

"Oh, I don't know. It's just that . . ." Binky paused to think. "I'd almost decided to ask this guy to send me a picture, then I realized that if I did that, he might ask me to send one to him."

"And what's so bad about that?"

"I'm not pretty like you. I'm just ordinary. Maybe he'd lose interest and quit talking to me."

"Binky, you are pretty. You're darling, and if you don't think so, ask Todd or Harry!"

"That's the other thing," Binky admitted. "I do kind of have a boyfriend, even if he is away at school most of the time. I would feel crummy being unfaithful to him. It's just this guy on the Internet is so nice. . . ."

"Frankly, Binky, I think that if a guy would judge you on the basis of one picture, he isn't worth bothering with. You know that."

Binky seemed to agree with Lexi's words. But Lexi wasn't so sure that they had sunk in. "If he doesn't like you for your mind and your personality, don't bother with him, Bink." Only Binky could manage to have romance troubles with a guy she'd never met!

Chapter Nine

Dmitri and Todd were in Mike's garage when Lexi and Binky found them. Lexi was relieved to see the guys laughing and joking as they worked. That was what she and Binky needed today—light-heartedness. For some reason, Binky had rung her doorbell this afternoon, come inside, and proceeded to mope around as though she'd lost her best friend. Puzzled by Binky's behavior but unable to get Binky to explain what was wrong, Lexi had finally resorted to suggesting that they go find the guys. Binky refused to go home, refused to tell Lexi what was wrong, and refused to be pleasant. It was highly uncharacteristic behavior, and it was driving Lexi crazy.

"Hi, guys, having fun?" Lexi greeted them.

Todd looked up from the engine he had his head buried in. There was a smudge of grease on his nose. "I'm just teaching Dmitri a thing or two about carburetors."

"Do you have a car?" Lexi asked Dmitri.

"No—although my family has one. Most families in Greece only have one car, unlike Americans, who seem to have many. Besides, I'm not old enough to drive yet."

"But you're seventeen," Binky said.

"That is right, but the legal age for driving in Greece is eighteen, and since cars are usually imported, expensive, and very heavily taxed, my father is not eager for me to start driving."

"Bummer," Binky said.

"Oh, it is not so bad. After all, you have to remember that Greece is a number of islands. Much of our travel is done by sea."

"Oh, I remember. You talked about those little boats—caïques."

"Yes, they are little boats that are pointed at each end, and they run between the mainland and the islands and between the islands themselves. We also use buses a great deal. It is a very practical and economical way to get around. When traveling in the mountains, though, riding in a bus can be a scary experience. The roads are narrow and the cliffs are steep. They are usually unprotected by barriers, so sometimes you feel as though you are crawling along the edge of the world."

"So if the villagers don't have cars and they don't have buses, how do the people up in the mountains get around?" Todd asked.

Dmitri smiled widely. "Often they use donkeys."

"You mean they use donkeys like we use four-wheelers or minibikes?"

Dmitri laughed. "Exactly."

"I think I'd like Greece," Binky said. "But I'm not sure about those donkeys."

Changing the subject, Lexi turned to Dmitri.

"Well, how was your date last night?"

Dmitri continued to smile widely. "I had a very nice time. Thank you," he said politely.

"And how did you like Minda?"

Smile lines crinkled around his eyes. "I liked her very much. She was a lot of fun."

"Was she crabby or bossy?" Binky asked.

"No, not at all. We went to a very funny movie. Then we had root beer floats before going to the party at her friend's house."

"And how was that?" Todd asked.

"We did not stay long. Minda seemed uncomfortable there."

"Because all the other girls were flirting with Dmitri, I'll bet," Binky whispered to Lexi.

"So we took a drive around the city and then went to Todd's house. Everyone was already in bed, so Minda and I watched a late-night movie, then she went home."

"Will wonders never cease," Binky said. "Minda sounding nice and normal—can you believe it?"

"Are you going to go out with her again?" Todd asked with a sly expression on his face.

"I do not know," Dmitri said honestly. "I have been very confused. I like both Minda and Jennifer. I talked to your mother about it, Todd, and she recommended—how do you Americans say it?—'playing the field.' Since I don't have too much time left here in America, she said that I should get to know as many people as I can."

"I'm not sure that's what Minda has in mind," Lexi said.

"Relationships are very complicated," Dmitri said with a sigh.

A choking sound turned everyone's attention to Binky. They were all surprised to see that there were tears running down her cheeks, and she was vainly trying to hold them back.

"Binky, what's wrong?" Lexi moved toward her friend. "You were fine a minute ago."

"I've done something terrible," Binky sobbed. "And if I tell you what it is, you'll never forgive me."

"What could you have done?" Todd said, puzzled. "You just got here."

"No, not now . . . before." Binky scrubbed at her eyes with her fists. "I've been feeling so guilty, and I didn't know how to tell anyone."

"We don't understand, Binky."

But Binky wouldn't, or couldn't, talk. Instead she sobbed, tears running down her cheeks, her face growing blotchy.

Finally, Todd's brother, Mike, came out of his office. "What's going on?"

"We don't know," Todd said. "Binky just started crying and said she's done something terrible. She won't tell us what it is."

"And she won't tell us what we can do to help her," Lexi added in frustration.

"Why don't you guys go into my office," Mike suggested. "There are some comfortable chairs in there."

They led a still-snuffling Binky into the office. She sat down on a straight-backed chair and took the wad of tissues that Lexi handed her.

When Binky's crying was somewhat under control, Lexi said softly, "What have you done that has upset you so much, Binky? Tell us. Maybe we can help you. Can it be undone?"

"No," Binky said, her voice trembling pitifully. "I can't get it back now. I can't believe I was so dumb."

"Can't get what back?" Todd asked.

Dmitri was watching the whole exchange with intense interest.

"I think my parents should take the computer out of our house," Binky said unexpectedly.

Lexi blinked. "So this has something to do with the computer?"

"It's so easy to get hooked on that thing," Binky complained. "And you type things because it feels so safe sitting in your room. But it's not really, is it?"

"I thought we had this conversation already," Todd said.

Binky looked at him with a bleary eye. "But it didn't sink in."

"Okay, Binky, you have to tell us—what have you done?"

"I met another guy on the Internet."

"Binky, you promised you weren't going to do that anymore."

"I know. I know. But it was just so neat to talk to that guy from Brentwood, I thought I'd try again. Everyone's really friendly. They sound really cool when they write about themselves. It's hard not to imagine them as all really great-looking, together guys."

"I don't like the sound of this," Todd muttered. "Spill it, Binky. What did you do?"

"Well, this guy asked for my picture." She paused, took a breath, and blurted, "And I sent one to him!"

"What's so bad about that? I wouldn't cry over that," Lexi soothed. "I'm glad you finally realized how cute you are. The way you were talking, it sounded as though you'd done something really dumb."

"But I did do something really dumb." Binky's voice grew tiny and fearful.

"What is it you're not telling us?" Todd demanded.

Binky looked at Lexi, then looked away. "I didn't send him my picture, I sent him Lexi's."

"You did *what*?" Lexi and Todd said in unison.

"He said I sounded really cute, and he was sure I was a really neat girl. He kept telling me how special I was, so I decided that I couldn't disappoint him. Then I looked at my school picture. You guys have all seen it—the one from last year. I forgot they were taking pictures that day, and I went to school with bad hair and an old flannel shirt on. Half of my bangs were going east, and the other half were going south. I was late that morning, remember? If you look real close at the picture, you can even see the lines on my face from where I was sleeping on my pillow."

"It wasn't that bad," Lexi protested.

"Yes, it was, Lexi Leighton, and you know it. And somewhere in my mind I decided that I just couldn't let that picture go floating around. Yours was lying right there next to it, so I just picked that one up and dropped it in the envelope." She hung her head. "Now I feel really dumb because he wrote back to me. I got the letter this morning. He thinks I'm 'adorable,' and he'd really like to get to know me better." She looked at Lexi pleadingly. "He's asked me to send more pictures."

"No, you don't," Lexi said firmly. "You are *not* sending some stranger pictures of me. Not only that, you're going to have to 'fess up right away. You're not a deceitful or dishonest person, Binky. I don't know what you were thinking of."

"I don't, either." Binky looked puzzled. "I think that the Internet is frying my brain."

"Well, before it's totally fried, you have to contact that person and tell him there will be no more pictures and that it's not even you."

"Oh, Lexi, do I have to? It's so embarrassing. I'll just quit writing to him."

"Sorry, that's not good enough," Lexi said. "You're going to tell him what you've done. I'll help you write the letter."

"Where is my brain when I need it?" Binky muttered. "If I'd use my head, I'd never get myself into these messes."

Lexi rummaged through the papers on top of Mike's desk and came up with a notepad and a pen. "We're going to sit down right now and decide what you're going to say. And, Binky, you're going to ask for my picture back."

"Oh, Lexi . . ."

Todd motioned to Dmitri and they left the office. Todd was shaking his head and laughing.

"Do you know, Todd," Dmitri said, "that I think

Americans are the most interesting people I have ever met?"

Todd turned to him with a grin on his face. "I can do better than that, Dmitri. Binky McNaughton is the most interesting human being *anyone* has ever met!"

———

"I want to talk to you, Golden." Minda stood at the far end of the hall in a stance that reminded Lexi of an old-time gunslinger facing off a shoot-out.

"Me? Why? You never have before." Jennifer eyed the other girl coolly.

"You know perfectly well 'why.' "

"No, I don't. Tell me."

"Dmitri isn't going to be here very much longer," Minda said bluntly. "I don't want you taking up any more of his time."

"When did he become your property?"

Minda glared at her, but Jennifer didn't back down.

Lexi leaned against the locker, hugging her books and watching. This was going to be interesting.

"Dmitri feels something special for me," Minda informed her.

"Really? Me too."

Concern flitted across Minda's features before they grew confident again. "Hah!"

"We're *friends*, Minda. And nothing you say or do can take that away."

Minda didn't seem to know how to react. Jennifer's statement was true. Minda had managed to spark Dmitri's interest, but she hadn't been able to separate Dmitri from Todd, Lexi, Jennifer, and the rest of the group. It must have been very frustrating for a girl who usually got her own way.

Minda tossed back her blond hair. "Just so you know where we stand." Her head held high, she stalked away.

Jennifer stared after Minda with a thoughtful expression on her face. Lexi remained silent, not knowing what to say. She did step forward, however, when she saw a tear slide down one of Jennifer's cheeks.

"Oh, Jen, don't let her get to you like that! She doesn't know everything about Dmitri's feelings!"

"No, probably not. Minda's not exactly Miss Sensitive. But I *do* know how he feels."

"You do?" Lexi couldn't keep the disbelief out of her voice.

"It's like I told Minda. Dmitri and I are *friends*. We've talked about it."

"He *told* you he likes Minda more than he likes you? That doesn't sound like him."

"He only said it because I pushed him into it. I wanted to know where I stood. I thought maybe I had a chance with him and that Minda was only confusing things. But I had it the other way around. I shouldn't be surprised. Minda's a much better flirt than I am. He said that she was something 'unique' and 'special' but that I was his 'dear friend.'"

"Ouch." Lexi winced. "Sometimes being a friend is second best, huh?"

Jennifer sighed and her shoulders sagged. "At

first that's what I thought. Then I realized that maybe, in this case, it was the very best thing to be. Dmitri is going away soon. Long-distance romances—especially halfway around the world—can't be easy to maintain. But friendships can. Letters. Phone calls. Happy memories. I wouldn't want to be loyal to only one guy if I didn't think I'd get to see him for at least a year. I'm too young for that."

"And Minda's not the loyal type, anyway, so it won't bother her?" Lexi deduced.

"Exactly. If Dmitri and I are meant to be more than friends, it's a long way into the future. But for now I have the best of both worlds."

"I am so proud of you," Lexi said. Her eyes were bright when she looked at her friend. "You sound so mature and *smart*!"

Jennifer gave an astonished grin. "Wow, I hardly ever get called smart. I like it."

"Then you don't feel too badly about Dmitri and Minda?"

"I'll get over it," Jennifer said eventually. "Maybe we should get the others together and go over to Todd's now."

———

"What was that all about today? I heard you and Minda had a little confrontation," Binky said to Jennifer as they neared Todd's house with Egg, Lexi, Peggy, and Matt.

"She was just making sure I don't crowd her and Dmitri," Jennifer said with a sly grin. "I know Dmitri likes her, and I can deal with that. But at least

I make Minda nervous where he's concerned." She winked at Lexi.

"You girls are hopeless," Egg said calmly as he punched the doorbell. "I'll never figure you out."

Todd opened the door before Egg could say more. He looked surprised to see everyone outside.

"Hi," Egg said as he stepped into the house. "We thought we'd come here and hang out for a while. Dmitri doesn't have much time left, so we'd like to visit with him."

"It's hard to believe that it's soon going to be time for you to leave," Jennifer observed. "It seems like you just got here."

"I agree," Dmitri said. "I already know that I will come back to America someday for a visit or perhaps to go to school again. I love your country, and I love the people, too."

"All this is too sad," Binky said.

A grin spread across Dmitri's face. "But I have had news from my mother. We have a computer at home now. So we can keep in touch by e-mail!"

Binky suddenly turned pale. "Don't say e-mail in front of me," she ordered. Then she brightened. "But I will write to you, Dmitri, and only you—well, and probably still Harry."

"What about Minda?" Jennifer asked. There was a hesitation in her voice.

Dmitri gave a small smile. "Oh yes. I will definitely keep in touch with her." Then he touched Jennifer's hand. "And you, too, if you will let me."

Jennifer's eyes glowed.

"Well, I think that's great," Egg said loudly. "Because Minda's been a whole lot nicer lately, and I think it's you that made her happy, Dmitri. I just hope that when you leave, she doesn't turn back into her old sour, grouchy, snobby self."

Chapter Ten

"I can't believe it's already here," Todd murmured as he put cans of soda into a chest full of ice. "The past few weeks just disappeared." He was referring to Dmitri's last day at Cedar River.

"When does his flight leave?" Lexi asked. She was dumping peanuts into serving dishes.

"He catches a plane to New York tomorrow morning. Then he flies directly to Athens, nonstop."

"Did you see Binky today?" Lexi asked.

"You mean 'Rudolph, our red-nosed classmate'?" Todd said, looking amused. "I didn't realize she'd gotten quite so attached to Dmitri. She's been crying like it's Egg that's leaving for Greece."

"I don't think it's all about Dmitri," Lexi confessed. "She told me that she'd told her Internet friend about sending him the wrong picture."

"Everything feels . . . strange, unsettled. Dmitri is leaving. Minda's moping around because he's leaving. Angela is acting weird and won't tell anyone what's going on with her. . . ."

"I know what you mean. I'm glad your mother is having a going-away party for Dmitri. We *need* a party." She looked up as the doorbell rang. "Sounds like it's about to start."

Dmitri was behaving like the perfect host in the living room, making sure everyone had a soda and a place to sit.

"Are you nervous?" Lexi asked him.

"I just want everything to be right tonight. I will miss these people." He looked over the group. Some were studying Todd's CDs, others were cheering on a video game between Tim and Jerry. Dmitri drifted through the groups, studying them intently, as if he were trying to memorize every face, every gesture.

"He's been doing that all night, hasn't he?" Todd asked Lexi later, inclining his head toward Dmitri.

"Looking as though he's trying to capture the moment in his mind, you mean? Yes. I didn't realize it would be so hard for him to leave. I know we'll miss him, but he has that beautiful country and his family and friends to return to—"

"I have a request," Mrs. Winston said, drawing attention to her side of the room. She held a video camera in her hand. "I still haven't made a video tape of the Greek dancing Dmitri showed us. How about it, guys, will you all join Dmitri?"

By the time they were through dancing, everyone was laughing and sitting around the living room, talking about the next party they were going to have so they could do some more Greek dancing.

Dmitri cleared his throat. "Excuse me, excuse me . . ."

Gradually the room quieted. All eyes turned to Dmitri.

"I want to thank you," he began, "for welcoming

me to your country and to your school. In these short weeks, you have become my friends. And the Winstons have become my family."

Binky snuffled. Minda dabbed daintily at her eye with a paper napkin. Jennifer sighed.

"I would like to extend an invitation to all of you to come to Greece and visit me and my family."

"Have you got enough room for all of us?" Tim asked. "All at once?"

"We'll make room!" Dmitri said with a huge grin. "I want to see *all* of you again."

———

"Things just don't feel right without Dmitri," Binky complained. The girls—including Minda—had gathered at Lexi's house to study. "I wish he'd come back."

"I wish I could go over *there*," Peggy blurted. "That's what I wish!"

"You can. I'm going to," Lexi said with conviction.

"With what money?"

"The money I earn once I get out of college and get a good job. Maybe I'll even go before I leave college—on a work-study program. There's no reason we can't travel."

"True, but not everyone can afford it," Binky pointed out.

"I think you can *make* opportunities, Binky. Study. College. Goals. If travel is one of your goals, you can work to make it happen." Lexi got a far-away look in her eye. "I want to see the places where Paul preached and where John the Evangelist took Mary, the mother of Jesus, after He ascended into heaven."

"Lexi's right," Jennifer said. "The world isn't just Cedar River or the United States. It's got lots of interesting people and fascinating cultures. I think I'd like to go to China. I'd see the Great Wall and—"

"Norway and Ireland!" Peggy said. "That's where I'd go."

"And miss *Paris*?" Minda looked shocked. "That's where all the fashion shows are held. That's where I want to go. Maybe I'll even be a designer."

"I'd like to go to Italy," Anna Marie murmured. "I hear they have great pasta in Italy."

As the girls speculated about where they would go and what they would see, Lexi began to realize what a wonderful gift Dmitri had given them—a taste of the world out there to be discovered.

Lexi smiled to herself. She was perfectly sure of one thing: Whenever any of them traveled in the years to come, Greece would always be on the list.

Quiet, sincere, and always sweet, Angela Hardy seems like the least likely person to cause trouble. But almost without warning, her behavior begins to change. Lexi and the gang are at the end of their ropes trying to get to the bottom of Angela's problem. But the rope snaps when Angela suddenly runs away. Her friends comb Cedar River from top to bottom, fearing the worst. But even if they find her, can they persuade her to come home? Find out in CEDAR RIVER DAYDREAMS #27.

A Note From Judy

I'm glad you're reading *Cedar River Daydreams*! I hope I've given you something to think about as well as a story to entertain you. If you feel you have any of the problems that Lexi and her friends experience, I encourage you to talk with your parents, a pastor, or a trusted adult friend. There are many people who care about you!

I love to hear from my readers, so if you'd like to receive my newsletter and a bookmark, please send a self-addressed, stamped envelope to:

Judy Baer
Bethany House Publishers
11300 Hampshire Avenue South
Minneapolis, MN 55438

———

Be sure to watch for my *Dear Judy . . .* books at your local bookstore. These books are full of questions that you, my readers, have asked in your letters, along with my response. Just about every topic is covered—from dating and romance to friendships and parents. Hope to hear from you soon!

Dear Judy, What's It Like at Your House?
Dear Judy, Did You Ever Like a Boy
   (who didn't like you?)

Live! From Brentwood High

Other Books by Judy Baer

Teen Series From
Bethany House Publishers

Early Teen Fiction (11–14)

HIGH HURDLES by Lauraine Snelling
Show jumper DJ Randall strives to defy the odds and achieve her dream of winning Olympic Gold.

SUMMERHILL SECRETS by Beverly Lewis
Fun-loving Merry Hanson encounters mystery and excitement in Pennsylvania's Amish country.

THE TIME NAVIGATORS by Gilbert Morris
Travel back in time with Danny and Dixie as they explore unforgettable moments in history.

Young Adult Fiction (12 and up)

CEDAR RIVER DAYDREAMS by Judy Baer
Experience the challenges and excitement of high school life with Lexi Leighton and her friends—over one million books sold!

GOLDEN FILLY SERIES by Lauraine Snelling
Readers are in for an exhilarating ride as Tricia Evanston races to become the first female jockey to win the sought-after Triple Crown.

JENNIE MCGRADY MYSTERIES by Patricia Rushford
A contemporary Nancy Drew, Jennie McGrady's sleuthing talents promise to keep readers on the edge of their seats.

LIVE! FROM BRENTWOOD HIGH by Judy Baer
When eight teenagers invade the newsroom, the result is an action-packed teen-run news show exploring the love, laughter, and tears of high school life.

THE SPECTRUM CHRONICLES by Thomas Locke
Adventure and romance await readers in this fantasy series set in another place and time.

SPRINGSONG BOOKS by various authors
Compelling love stories and contemporary themes promise to capture the hearts of readers.

WHITE DOVE ROMANCES by Yvonne Lehman
Romance, suspense, and fast-paced action for teens committed to finding pure love.